The tip you give in a restaurant comes
from the phrase "To Insure Prompt Service."
NOT SO!

New York City is the largest city in the U.S.A.
NO WAY!

The cheetah is the world's fastest animal.
UNTRUE!

The Brooklyn Dodgers got their name from their
agility.
YOU GOTTA BE KIDDING!

Bagpipes were invented in Scotland.
GUESS AGAIN

The above is just a sampling of the massive mis-
conceptions blown away by a book that tells you
everything from who invented the condom to how
Oprah got her name, and from why flies dodge
blows so well to why pirates wore earrings. Now
you can find out what fun it is to discover how
little you know, and how much you can learn, in
the ultimate treasury of oddball information and
freaky facts.

THE UNBELIEVABLE TRUTH!
*The perfect gift for every
know-it-all*

THE
UNBELIEVABLE
Truth!

by

Jeff Rovin

A SIGNET BOOK

SIGNET
Published by the Penguin Group
Penguin Books USA Inc., 375 Hudson Street,
New York, New York 10014, U.S.A.
Penguin Books Ltd, 27 Wrights Lane,
London W8 5TZ, England
Penguin Books Australia Ltd, Ringwood,
Victoria, Australia
Penguin Books Canada Ltd, 10 Alcorn Avenue,
Toronto, Ontario, Canada M4V 3B2
Penguin Books (N.Z.) Ltd, 182–190 Wairau Road,
Auckland 10, New Zealand

Penguin Books Ltd, Registered Offices:
Harmondsworth, Middlesex, England

First published by Signet,
an imprint of Dutton Signet,
a division of Penguin Books USA Inc.

First Printing, August, 1994
10 9 8 7 6 5 4 3 2 1

PUBLISHER'S NOTE
This is a work of fiction. Names, characters, places, and incidents either are the product of the author's imagination or are used fictitiously, and any resemblance to actual persons, living or dead, events, or locales is entirely coincidental.

BOOKS ARE AVAILABLE AT QUANTITY DISCOUNTS WHEN USED TO PROMOTE PRODUCTS OR SERVICES. FOR INFORMATION PLEASE WRITE TO PREMIUM MARKETING DIVISION, PENGUIN BOOKS USA INC., 375 HUDSON STREET, NEW YORK, NEW YORK 10014.

Introduction

In 1775, Samuel Johnson wrote, "Knowledge is of two kinds. We know a subject ourselves, or we know where we can find information upon it."

These days, what we don't experience firsthand we can find in any number of places. Information comes at us from every direction and every medium, though unfortunately, much of it is related to business or school or running a household. There's not enough fun in what we learn.

The Unbelievable Truth! strives to change that. It's packed with facts of all kinds, from entertainment to food to history to biology. It answers questions you may have always wondered about, and will give you something to spring on your colleagues during a lull in your next business lunch or on your friends at a dull party.

Most of all, we hope this book will fascinate you and make you hungry for more. For as Aldous Huxley said, "If a little knowledge is dangerous, where is the man who has so much as to be out of danger?"

Animals

The term "greyhound" originally had nothing to do with the dog's color. It came from the old Norse term "groy," meaning "bitch," and was applied to any female dog. Later, when the word traveled to England, it was used to describe just the dog of that color. Even later, in the U.S., the term gave the busline its name (see entry for "Greyhound Corporation," p. 25).

For the record, greyhounds have the keenest eyesight of any dog breed.

• ■ •

Unlike "greyhound," the expression "raining cats and dogs" did, originally, mean exactly that. As far back as the sixteenth century, cats and some dogs would do their hunting on London rooftops. During downpours, the animals would be washed from gutters and over eaves, inspiring the popular euphemism for a cloudburst.

• ■ •

Lots of dead cats resulted from downpours, but contrary to popular belief, catgut never came from cats.

It was made from the washed, cut, and stretched intestines of sheep. Used to make musical instruments, they produced a sound like a cat's squeals, hence the name.

• ■ •

While we're on the subject of cats, lions are the only felines that live together naturally. Zoologists have no idea why, since tigers, cheetahs, and other big cats don't hunt in packs. They suspect environmental reasons played a part in forcing the lions to cooperate.

• ■ •

Bats aren't blind. Their erratic flight patterns, plus the fact that they fly at dusk, suggested to early peoples that they had terrible vision. Quite the opposite is true; they have excellent eyesight. They fly helter-skelter because they chase darting bugs through the dark sky.

Bats are, however, disoriented in sudden brightness because their eyes are accustomed to the dark. In some countries, the phrase is not "blind as a bat" but "blind as a bat in sunlight."

In addition to possessing sharp eyesight, bats emit high-pitched sounds which work like sonar to help them navigate in the dark.

• ■ •

Other winged creatures have surprising reasons for what they do as well. Birds don't fly in a "V" formation to keep from losing members, or to present a daunting figure to potential predators. They do it because it helps them stay aloft. The flapping of the lead bird generates an updraft that helps the second row of birds, and so on down the line. The lead birds change positions regularly, which allows them to increase their effective range by sixty to seventy percent.

• ■ •

Vultures aren't migrators, but they're unique in another way: they're bald in order to stay healthy. The birds tend to stick their beaks into places where all kinds of mites and bacteria exist. Since the birds have no feathers on top, there's nothing for these potentially dangerous life forms to cling to.

• ■ •

The penguin is also designed as it is for a reason. In fact, it's one of nature's most cleverly camouflaged creatures. Seen from above, the animal's black back resembles the dark sea. When a predator spots a penguin from below the waves, the gray-white vest makes the bird look like a patch of sky.

Unlike most birds, penguins don't have hollow bones. They need the weight for ballast.

• ■ •

With all the pigeons one sees in our cities, it's surprising that there don't seem to be any baby pi-

geons. They're around, all right; we just can't see them.
Pigeons are relatively helpless until they're about a
month old. Only then do they venture from under aw-
nings, ledges, and from treetops to join the general
pigeon population.

• ■ •

Since peacocks don't lay eggs, how do we get more
of them? From peahens. As their name implies, peacocks are the males of the peafowl family.

Incidentally, cocker spaniels got their name from
being used to hunt peacocks and other cock-birds.

• ■ •

The cheetah may be the world's fastest land animal,
able to run just over seventy miles an hour for short
periods, but it isn't the world's fastest animal by a long
shot. That honor goes to the peregrine falcon, which
can dive at speeds of up to 240 miles an hour.

And no, gravity doesn't help as much as you'd think:
the bird can rocket upward at just over half that speed.

• ■ •

And which animal is the world's slowest? The three-
toed sloth, whose top speed is a less-than-blistering
eight feet a minute.

• ■ •

Speaking of speed, porpoises and dolphins jump from the water only when they're in a hurry. They encounter less resistance in the air than in the sea.

•　■　•

Sperm whales did not get their names because they resemble individual sperm cells. Rather, early whalers thought the gel-like substance in their snouts was the seed of the whale, i.e., spermaceti. Not so. Its primary function is to cushion the whale's sensitive snout as it dives.

•　■　•

In that respect, elephants are more rugged than whales; apart from humans, they're the only animals that can learn to stand on their head.

•　■　•

And elephants aren't really afraid of mice. The myth arose from an ancient Greek story about a mouse crawling up an elephant's trunk and driving it mad. But if the incident happened, it was isolated and rare. Elephants ignore mice and other small creatures. They only show fear in the face of recognized predators: large cats, dogs, and humans, in that order.

•　■　•

Camels can go from eight days to eight weeks without water. However, this is not because their humps are hollow. It's because camels sweat and urinate very little. Water is absorbed into the camel's body and literally recycled. At the same time, the camel's metabolic rate slows as needed, rationing the water. In extreme heat, the camel keeps cool due to the high water content of its blood.

The fat stored in the camel's hump provides energy when the animal is deprived of nourishment. The hump also absorbs the sun's direct rays, cooling them and protecting the organs below.

• ■ •

Plants are not placed in home aquaria for decoration. They provide oxygen for your pet fish. That's one reason goldfish in a gravel-filled bowl die young.

Believe it or not, the average lifespan of a goldfish is seven years—albeit perhaps not in your experience.

• ■ •

Though Groundhog Day is supposed to give us some indication about the proximity of spring, the emergence of groundhogs from their burrows has nothing to do with the weather. They come out to eat and mate. Perhaps that explains why their predictions have been wrong 72 percent of the time!

• ■ •

Big, insincere tears in a person are called "crocodile tears." But what are crocodile tears in a crocodile? They're glandular secretions produced to wash salt from the reptile's eyes. Crocodiles have no tear ducts.

Incidentally, the difference between alligators and crocodiles is geographical—alligators live only in the southeastern U.S. and in China—and in the shape of their snouts, which are broader and rounder in alligators.

• ■ •

Snakes dart their tongues in order to find prey. The reptile's tongue can literally taste the spoor of an animal that has passed by, and unerringly tracks it down. The tongue is also extremely sensitive to vibrations and can tell when and where an animal is moving.

• ■ •

And finally, Mother Carey's chickens, another name for small seabirds, have nothing to do with some gray-haired farm lady. They're named after *mater cara*, the Virgin Mother, who was believed to watch over sailors through her doting birds.

Art

The painting popularly known as "Whistler's Mother" was not called that by the artist. James McNeill Whistler named the work, "Arrangement in Gray and Black: the Artist's Mother."

Whistler's painting is the only one by an American hanging in the Louvre in Paris.

• ■ •

Likewise, Auguste Rodin's famous sculpture commonly called "The Thinker" isn't that at all. It's a statue of the poet Dante Alighieri. Rodin was a great admirer of the Italian poet and his allegorical epic the *Divine Comedy*.

The work was given its name by a dubious (and, thankfully, unknown) art critic who had never heard of Alighieri.

• ■ •

And though we call it the "Mona Lisa," Leonardo da Vinci's painting is actually titled "La Giaconda." It's a portrait of Lisa Gherardini, the wife of Florentine merchant Francesco del Giacondo. According to X rays of the work, which was painted on wood, Leonardo sketched three different poses before settling on the final design.

Lisa, incidentally, has no eyebrows because it was the style for women at the time to shave them off. No one knows who started the craze or why. (In case you want to try it yourself, think before you raze; eyebrows take three months to grow back.)

• ■ •

Cutting off a portion of his ear on Christmas Eve, 1888, had nothing to do with Vincent van Gogh's mental imbalance. He was suffering from a severe ear infection and *that* drove him to distraction. He felt better when the amputation was finished, largely because he'd passed out.

When he came to, Van Gogh wrapped the severed section of ear and presented it to a prostitute named Rachel. She wasn't fond of his paintings, and he wanted to show her that there were worse things he could give her. He was right. Thinking the package contained a Christmas present, Rachel opened it and promptly fainted.

• ■ •

It is traditional that if a statue of a horse has all four hooves on the ground, the rider died of natural causes. If one hoof is raised, death was due to wounds sustained in battle, and if two hooves are in the air, the rider died on the battlefield.

Automobiles

Henry Ford didn't invent the car. He took the inventions of Gottlieb Daimler and Karl Benz of Germany and Charles Edgar Duryea of the U.S., among others, and refined them. What he *did* do was produce the most popular car of its day: the Model T, which sold for $850 in 1908 and dropped to $290 by 1924. The "T" stood for nothing except the fact that it followed the Model S.

Benz was the inventor of the automobile, achieving a top speed of ten miles an hour with his first car in 1886.

• ■ •

Henry Ford did not introduce the assembly line to the manufacture of automobiles, either. Ransom E. Olds did, in 1901, increasing his factory's output from 425 cars that year to 2,500 the next. Ford simply improved on the idea, speeding production of the Model T from a day and a half to an hour and a half.

• ■ •

Why was the "T" known as the Tin Lizzie? Because Lizzie was a common nickname for household domestics, who worked hard all week then went to church on weekends. The Model T did likewise and thus became a family's Tin Lizzie.

The Model T was the bestselling autombile in history until 1972, when Volkswagen's Beetle surpassed it.

• ■ •

The first car with air-conditioning was the Packard: the option was perfected in November, 1939, and was sold to the public the following year. It was nearly 20 years before the extra was inexpensive and effective enough to make it a common option.

The first automobile to have seat belts was the 1950 Nash Rambler.

• ■ •

The "Mercedes" of Mercedes-Benz is not one of the founders, investors, or an inventor of anything. It was the name of the daughter of Emil Jellinek, a wealthy Austrian who hired Daimler's firm to design a car for him in 1900. Emil dubbed the car Mercedes (as he had his two other racing cars), a name he and Benz continued to use when their companies merged in 1926.

• ■ •

The British drive on the left side of the road because of the way they used to drive their coaches. Coachmen used to sit on the right because that was the side on which the riders entered, women first, men second. The coachmen had to be nearer the man to hear any instructions. He kept the carriage to the left so his whip wouldn't strike pedestrians. In most other countries, gallantry took a back seat to public safety and the men entered first, keeping the coachman on the left.

Swedes were the other notable left-side drivers, though they finally made the switch to the right side in September, 1967.

• ■ •

Why do we drive on a parkway and park in a driveway? Because as originally conceived, a parkway was a road that ran through and around a park, while a driveway was a circular roadway by which we drove past a house.

The Bible and Religion

Nowhere in the Bible does it say, "Pride goeth before a fall," as is commonly misquoted. What it says in Proverbs 16:18, is "Pride goeth before destruction, and an haughty spirit before a fall."

• ■ •

According to Talmudic scholars, people are different colors because the angel Azrael, whom God dispatched to collect the earth from which Adam was made, gathered it from different depths and locales. Adam's children, therefore, were all different colors.

Talmudists also report that Adam and Eve dwelt in Paradise a mere 12 hours before they were expelled.

• ■ •

What is the "skin of the teeth," and what does it mean to escape by it? In the Bible, Job 19:20, while recounting his myriad woes, Job says, "My bone cleaveth to my skin and to my flesh, and I am escaped with the skin of my teeth." In other words, he has been left with what little flesh remains on his bones and face.

• ■ •

The Bible does not say that money is the root of all
evil. What it says, in 1 Timothy 6:10 is, "For the
love of money is the root of all evil." Obviously, in and
of itself, money cannot be evil.

• ■ •

And certainly the author of the Bible did not exactly
say, in Isaiah 2:4, ". . . and they shall beat their
swords into plowshares . . ." The plowshare wasn't developed until some six hundred years after the birth of
Jesus, and only then in Europe, not in the Middle East.
The use of the word was the work of a later translator,
just as the Commandment "Thou shalt not murder"
was mistranslated as "Thou shalt not kill."

• ■ •

Because church officials did not know whether St.
Patrick was born on March 8th or 9th, they decided
to honor him on March 17th—the sum of the two
dates.

• ■ •

The Old Testament was originally written in an early
form of Hebrew, but what of the New Testament?
It was written in Greek. At the time, Greek, and not

Latin (of *course* not Latin, the language of the oppressive Romans) was considered the language of erudition.

• ■ •

It wasn't Delilah who cut Samson's hair. According to Judges 16:17–19, after Samson told her the secret of his strength, "she made him sleep upon her knees; and she called for a man, and she caused him to shave off the seven locks of his head." The barber used a razor, to which Samson had alluded a few lines before.

• ■ •

The Golden Rule, "All things whatsoever ye would that men should do to you, do ye even so to them" (St. Matthew 7:12), was given its name by English clergyman Clement Ellis in 1660. However, he did not choose "golden" because the rule shines like the metal. He called it golden because, unlike a leaden rule, it cannot be "so easily bent and made crooked, or melted and dissolved by the heat of passion."

Actually, gold *can* be melted easily, though Ellis may not have realized that.

• ■ •

The Gutenberg Bible was the first printed book, printed in Mainz, Germany in 1456. It wasn't printed on paper but on vellum, which is made of calfskin.

• ■ •

What was Potter's Field, and why were the destitute buried there? According to St. Matthew 27:7, it's the land that was purchased with the silver Judas left behind when he took his own life. It thus became the symbolic home of all who die alone and impoverished.

• ■ •

The "X" in Xmas does not stand for the cross, and is not intended to keep the name of Christ from being used in a frivolous and unholy way. Quite the opposite. The Greek word for Christ, *Xristos*, from which the English word derives, begins with the letter *chi*, or "X", making the substitution both accurate and reverent.

• ■ •

"Jumping Jehoshaphat" derives from the ninth-century B.C. king of Judah who, in 1 Kings 22:48, lost his fleet in a storm in the Gulf of Akaba. When he heard the news, he leapt and screamed wildly, hence, the expression.

• ■ •

Roman Catholic clergymen were not forbidden to marry until 385 A.D., when Pope Siricius decreed that it would be a good discipline for bishops, priests, and deacons. Those who were married at the time were expected to separate. Many did not agree and left the priesthood.

Ironically, the first Pope, Peter, was himself a husband.

• ■ •

April Fool's day was originally held to honor the first journey of the dove from Noah's Ark. Noah expected it to find dry land and it found none. Revelers, dressed as the beasts of the ark, re-created the event by playing tricks on one another.

Business and Commerce

Many people believe that it's illegal to deface U.S. currency. It isn't. What's illegal is defacing it and then trying to spend it.

In any case, the government will replace destroyed money if three/fifths of it is still identifiable. Two/fifths will earn the bearer half the face value; less than that gets nothing.

• ■ •

Until the one-hundredth anniversary of Abraham Lincoln's birth, there wasn't a coin one could deface, as it were. That was when the first U.S. portrait-coin, the Lincoln penny, was issued.

What all coins have had, portrait or no, is a design with some symbol of liberty on it.

• ■ •

The world's first and oldest airline, KLM, began carrying passengers in 1920. The Dutch airline's first flights were between Amsterdam and London.

• ■ •

In August of 1914, eager to pick up some extra cash, Minnesotan Carl Wickman used his big gray car to drive miners to and from their huts to the mines. Though he only had room for a half-dozen passengers, he found himself hauling as many as 20 miners a trip. Encouraged, he bought a bigger car and founded the Greyhound Corporation.

• ■ •

If the person who handles corporate accounts is a controller, why do we call him or her a comptroller? Because around 1500, someone mistook the French word *compte,* or "count" (as in nobility), for "count" (in reference to money). The name stuck, though both it and controller are correct and are pronounced the same.

• ■ •

When Charles Louis Tiffany opened his original store on Broadway in September, 1837, his bread-and-butter was stationery. Later, he diversified into what he called "fancy goods," including flatware, crystal, clocks, and, because he had a little room left over in one display case, jewelry.

• ■ •

The famous Lloyd's of London was never an insur-
ance company but an organization of underwriters
who issue policies individually or, at times, in tandem.
Nothing ever was or could be insured by Lloyd's of
London, per se.

• ■ •

The use of "Ltd." (Limited) in British corporations is
not synonymous with "Inc." or "Co." or any similar
descriptions. Rather, it means that the liability of each
stockholder is limited to the sum he or she has
invested.

Clothing and Fashion

Panama hats are not made in Panama, and never were. They originated in Ecuador in the 19th century. They were sent north to Panama, from where they were shipped around the world.

• ■ •

In 1886, young Griswold Lorillard of the tobacco family, went to a party at a New York country club. He hated swallow-tailed coats, however, and had his dinner jacket designed without tails. Though people gasped, at first, at his informality, the suit he was wearing became a more comfortable alternative for men. It was also named after the location of the party: Tuxedo Park, New York.

• ■ •

Many people assume that the G-string was named after the heavy violin string it resembles. Many dictionaries also make that error.

In fact, the "G" stands for groin, and the term was first used in the 18th century, in the name of decency, when describing the skimpy loincloths worn by American Indians.

Nowadays, no one using or observing a g-string is likely to be offended by the word "groin."

• ■ •

The necktie originated in Ancient Rome, where soldiers wore them to keep warm in the cold and to absorb sweat when it was hot. Later, European armies followed suit. During the French Revolution, neckties were worn by the general public, as men used the color of their necktie to signal their allegiance to the rebels or to the royalists.

Neckties moved from political statement to fashion item thereafter, often as the one place where a man could display flair or color in his otherwise drab attire.

The French necktie, or cravat, is named for *khrvat*, the Croatian military neckwear which inspired the French design.

• ■ •

Blazers also had a military origin, named for the smart jackets worn on the 19th-century British naval ship *HMS Blazer*. The blue jackets became a fashion craze in Britain and the U.S.

• ■ •

In 1760, blonde Countess Marie of Coventry, England, died of lead poisoning as a result of the excessive amount of makeup she used. Her death due to vanity gave rise to the popular notion that blondes are dumb.

• ■ •

The original Scottish kilts were nearly 15 feet long and worn as a matter of practicality. The people were poor, and the one garment could be used as a blanket, shawl, or small tent, and put to other uses as well. They also allowed the wearer to move with relative ease across the rocky, uneven land.

• ■ •

Diamonds are measured in carats, not ounces or fractions thereof, because of the ancient custom of weighing them using carob beans, which come from the *Ceratonia Siliqua* tree. Unlike other nuts and beans, carob beans are all nearly exactly the same weight, which made them a useful measure worldwide.

• ■ •

Dry cleaning isn't dry, really. The clothes are put in a large washing machine and treated with a variety of solutions, such as perchloroethylene, after which a drier removes the solvents. Tough stains are given personal attention, after which the clothing is pressed and folded.

Cleaned, yes. Dry-cleaned, no.

• ■ •

Nowadays, there are just six rivets in a pair of Levi's jeans. However, a century ago there were 501 little metal tabs. The company recently named a style of their jeans in honor of this.

• ■ •

Leather clothing that has wrinkles that can't be removed means the leather came from the neck or underside of the animal. During life, those parts are the tenderest; in death, they are neither tough nor resilient, so any creases they get become permanent.

• ■ •

Thanks to the copiousness of his belly, England's King Edward VII wasn't able to fasten the bottom button of his vests and jackets. By leaving them undone, he began a fashion trend which continues to this day.

• ■ •

The zoot suit originated during World War I. With the older men away, younger men were figuratively stepping into their shoes ... and their much bigger and baggier clothes. The fashion craze really boomed with the "hep-cats" of the 1930s.

The name had no meaning other than the trend, at that time, of rhyming words, as in "reet pleat" and "jeepers creepers."

• ■ •

Before Alexander the Great came to power, nary a man in Europe nor North Africa shaved. But young Alexander wasn't able to grow much of a beard and began the custom of scraping off his whiskers each day with a dagger. Naturally, those close to him did likewise, and soon it became the fashion.

• ■ •

In Ancient Rome, before anyone had pockets, the only place to hang a kerchief was from one's belt. These became known as "hang-kerchiefs." Years later, when the jackets of affluent Europeans covered up the waist, the kerchiefs were tucked in the cuffs and were called "handkerchiefs."

• ■ •

The only way your fly can be open is if your zipper is open as well. The zipper is the metal clasp and the fly is the flap of cloth that covers it.

• ■ •

The reason cowboy boots have high heels has nothing to do with being macho. They're made that way to keep the boot from slipping through the stirrup of a saddle. The stitching on the sides helps strengthen them.

• ■ •

Though high-heeled shoes originated with men who rode for a living, they were adapted by the general populace for one reason and one reason only: to keep peoples' feet out of muck, whether it was a gentleman walking to his carriage or a butcher slogging through blood. In the 18th century, as drainage improved, men gave up high heels altogether.

Customs and Symbols

Modern-day teenagers can thank the ancient Normans for having to wait until they're 21 before being considered "legal." In the middle of the 11th century, 13 was considered the legal age in Europe, the Middle East, and portions of Asia—legal for holding property and for serving in the military.

After suffering numerous casualties in their conquests, the Normans realized that 13-year-olds were simply not strong enough to carry armor and weapons, and 19 was made the legal age for war as well as inheritance. However, as the process of inheriting estates took two years, it wasn't long before the age of 21 came to mark the official beginning of adulthood.

• ■ •

The tradition of flying the flag at half-mast to honor the dead developed from the 16th-century practice of a ship lowering its flag to half-mast as a sign of submission to a foe. When the ship reached port, the flag remained half-raised as a mark of honor to those who fell in its defense. The tradition moved to land in the 17th century, as a sign of respect for one who has served his or her country beyond the call of duty.

• ■ •

The only public place where the U.S. flag is flown continuously is the Capitol Building in Washington, D.C. There are two of them, one on the east side, the other on the west side; they're only taken down when it's time to replace them with new flags.

• ■ •

In certain African nations, umbrellas have always been used to shade people from the sun and served as a tribute to the might of the sun god; opening them in the shade or inside a dwelling was considered an insult and certain to bring down the god's wrath. The custom moved to Spain in the 12th century and, today, it's still considered bad luck to open an umbrella indoors.

• ■ •

The idea that one could find a pot of gold at the end of a rainbow is a corruption of the original concept. In the 13th century, it was commonly said that one was as *likely* to find a pot of gold as to find the end of a rainbow. The expression was changed by the Irish, who adapted it to their fairy mythology.

• ■ •

How did R_x come to symbolize pharmacies? It came from the Romans and what they viewed as a mandate from their highest god to pursue medical research. The "R" comes from the Latin *recipere* ("to take"), while the "x" symbolizes Jupiter, who was both the king of the Roman gods and the god of medicine. As with the Greek Hippocratic oath, a Roman who used this symbol was devoted to the art of healing.

• ■ •

The derisive gesture of putting the thumbs in the ears and wiggling one's fingers originated in the Middle Ages as a way of telling a rival that he or she is a jackass.

Putting the fingers to the nose and wiggling comes to us from India and is a shorthand—or is it longhand?—way of calling someone an elephant.

• ■ •

The superstition that it's bad luck to walk under ladders arose from the executioner's use of a ladder to place a noose around the neck of the condemned—who, of course, was standing beneath it. People believed that anyone who passed under a ladder would meet the spirits of the evil dead, who were condemned to spend eternity there.

• ■ •

Spilling salt has been considered bad luck ever since Lot's hapless wife looked back on Sodom and Gomorrah and was turned into a pillar of it. Salt came to be regarded as *the* symbol of temptation, and spilling it was viewed as a means of summoning the ultimate tempter, the devil.

Once it was spilled and the devil was called, what was one to do? Throw some salt over one's shoulder, hoping to hit the devil in the eye and blind him while the salt was cleaned up.

The left shoulder had no significance other than the fact that most people were right-handed.

• ■ •

The first celebration in which ticker tape was thrown was the dedication of the Statue of Liberty on October 28, 1886. The ceremonies were visible from windows in buildings along Wall Street, and festive brokers impulsively tossed the ticker tape out the window.

The most ticker tape ever dropped was in New York, in 1981, for the hostages who had been freed from Iran. That parade produced 1,262 tons of tape. The runner-up was the parade honoring the world champion New York Mets in 1986. That one generated 648 tons.

• ■ •

The familiar symbol for peace was designed in 1958 by members of the Direct Action Committee, a nuclear disarmament group. The inverted Y-shaped design was created using the semaphore symbols for "N" and "D".

• ■ •

How did the rabbit's foot and not a dog's or cat's or pig's foot become a good-luck token?

The tradition dates back to at least 500 B.C., when the fecundity of the rabbit made it highly regarded (hence, too, its use as a symbol for springtime fertility which has come down to us as the modern-day Easter Bunny).

Initially, the entire pelt was considered lucky and was used to make various kinds of garments, from mittens to hats. In time, though, the foot was seen as symbolic of its powers, apparently due to its phallic shape.

• ■ •

The tradition that it's bad luck to light three cigarettes with one match dates back to World War I: keeping a light burning in the trenches gave the enemy enough time to aim and fire.

• ■ •

Who decided that boys should wear blue and girls should wear pink? Someone in England circa 1400. Since blue was the color of the sky—hence, of heaven and God—it was long thought to be a color that warded off evil spirits. Only boys were dressed in it, however, because girls were thought to be of no interest to demons. It took another hundred years before girls got their own color. The antithesis of blue, red, was considered too hot a color for girls, so the softer pink was used.

• ■ •

Speaking of colors, black became the color of mourning not because it reflected the dark mood of the mourners. Rather, it was believed that the spirits of the dead remained on earth for a time, searching for a familiar body to inhabit. By wearing black and walking in the shadows or staying indoors, mourners believed that they would not be seen.

• ■ •

The act of a man tipping his hat to a woman originated in the days when knighthood was in flower. Theoretically, a knight had nothing to fear in the presence of a lady, and would remove his helmet out of deference. Today, soldiers remove their hats in the presence of a superior officer for much the same reason.

• ■ •

The wearing of wedding rings has nothing to do with the fact that primitive tribes often captured women from neighboring tribes and brought them back in fetters. Rather, it dates back to the ancient Egyptian practice of sealing pacts with a mutual show of trust. Since the possession of a signet ring carried with it the proxy power of the owner, the ring became the symbol of that trust in government, in business, and in marriage.

The fourth finger of the left hand was selected as the ring finger in the third century B.C., because it was the starting point of what physicians believed was a nerve that ran directly to the heart.

• ▪ •

After marriage comes the honeymoon, which was so named by the Teutons, who celebrated a wedding by drinking honey mead each night from new moon to new moon.

In 1552, etymologist Richard Huloet suggested the term really means that love for one's honey wanes like the moon after marriage, though Huloet offered no historical basis for his definition. Presumably, personal experience had something to do with it.

• ▪ •

At some point after the honeymoon come babies, and it was the Norse who gave us the notion that babies are delivered by storks. Because storks frequently nested on warm chimneys and treated their young with kindness, they became symbolic figures of parenthood. They were also spotted making nests out of clothing plucked from clothes lines. Seeing them, one could easily imagine that they were stuffing babies down the flue.

This notion was popularized by the writings of Hans Christian Andersen ("The Storks"), among others.

The myth of finding babies in the cabbage patch derived from the fecundity of rabbits, who were regulars there (see the entry for "rabbit's foot," p. 37).

• ■ •

The custom of offering up a salutation before drinking came from the ancient Roman practice of dropping a small square of spiced toast into the beverage to soak up the sediment before drinking. A salutation was offered while the bread did its work; these so-called "toasts" were kept brief, though, lest the toast sit there too long and begin breaking up.

It was the custom for the host to present this toast and then take the first sip, to prove that the drink wasn't rancid or poisoned.

• ■ •

As far back as the tenth century, ships from the South Seas to the North Sea were christened using the blood of sacrificial victims. The thinking was that the spirit of the dead person would guide the craft safely over the waters.

Later, as sacrifices were frowned upon in many cultures, wine was used instead of blood. However, the church complained that wine symbolized the blood of Jesus, and it was eventually replaced by its bubbly relative, champagne.

• ■ •

The custom of executing condemned persons before sunrise began in ancient days, when human sacrifices—typically, prisoners—were offered to the rising sun. In the Middle Ages, executions were held early so they wouldn't attract too large a crowd, since, as the

French Revolution later proved, mobs of people tended to get bloodthirty and unruly after a beheading or two.

Today, prisons generally perform executions early in the day so as not to upset and arouse other convicts who might be still asleep.

• ■ •

A four-leaf clover is not regarded as lucky because it's rare. Rather, it's the leaf's resemblance to the cross that caused Europeans of the Middle Ages to regard it as a token of good luck.

Many people consider the three-leaf clover to be a representation of the Holy Trinity.

Entertainment

Why are bad shows called "turkeys"? Around the turn of the century, it became the habit for theaters in major cities to stage all plays between Thanksgiving and Christmas, just to capture a share of the tourist trade. This was referred to as "serving theatergoers turkey." By the mid-1940s, the word was being used alone to describe a show of little merit.

• ■ •

The phrase "stealing one's thunder" had its origin in the theater in 1709. Though playwright and critic John Dennis's play *Appius and Virginia* was a flop, the author came up with a novel setup of wooden troughs with hammerlike stops to produce thunderclaps of different volume. Shortly after his play closed, *Macbeth* opened at the same theater. Dennis attended in his capacity as a critic and was shocked to hear his thunder-making device being used.

"By God!" he wrote. "The villains will not play my play, but they steal my thunder!"

• ■ •

As far back as the 15th century, dancers were already acting out ballets, stories set to music. However, it wasn't until 1827, when a young, incredibly light, graceful Italian dancer, Marie Taglioni, got on the tips of her toes, that modern ballet was launched. And it wasn't until near the end of the century that her style of pointe work was taught in ballet classes; it took that long for teachers to figure out just how to do it, with the aid of sturdier shoes.

• ■ •

In Russia, where ballet is a way of life, *Bolshoi* ballet means "grand" ballet.

• ■ •

The Can-Can was introduced in Paris in 1858 and named after *canard*, French for duck. Why a duck? Because the object was for the dancers to display their tail feathers.

• ■ •

There really are snake charmers in India, and they really do charm snakes, including cobras. The art form dates back to the third century B.C. However, the charmers don't work their magic with music (snakes can't hear). It's the wind from the charmer's flute, as well as various hand and head gestures, that capture the snake's attention.

The real skill of the charmer is in keeping the reptile sufficiently intrigued without making it angry.

• ■ •

From the 16th through the 18th centuries, masked, costumed players in the Italian *commedia dell'arte* would improvise plotlines based on standard traits for their characters. The comic figure Harlequin typically hit the backsides of his bumbling associates using a piece of wood with another board fastened to it. The sound of wood striking wood gave us the term "slap-stick," meaning any kind of broad, silly comedy.

• ■ •

Most sword swallowers really do swallow swords. They learn their craft by stifling the gag reflex, usually starting out with cutlery, then moving on to daggers and small swords. If the body is properly aligned, the sword swallower can take a blade some two feet long. Since the sword will reach the stomach, it's important that the stomach be empty: regurgitation can be deadly.

• ■ •

When she was an actress in high school, Nancy Davis appeared in the play *First Lady*, in which she uttered the following line of dialogue: "They ought to elect the First Lady and then let her husband be President."

Ms. Davis later married fellow actor Ronald Reagan.

Food

Everyone knows that the Earl of Sandwich invented the sandwich in the middle of the 18th century. What most people don't know is that he came up with it because he was a compulsive gambler. He wanted to find a way of eating without leaving the gaming table, and the sandwich was the solution.

• ■ •

Chop suey did not originate in China but in San Francisco, circa 1860. The inventor was a Chinese dishwasher who would dice leftovers and mix them in a dish. At first, he'd eat them himself; after the restaurant owner sampled some, he decided to offer it to customers. It isn't known which of the men coined the name, or whether "chop" comes from "chopsticks" or the American "chop," to "cut up" or "mince." "Suey" is from the Chinese word *sui*, or "bits."

Over the next three decades, the dish made its way east. It was popularized in 1896 when a Chinese official, Li Hung-chang, was visiting New York during a world tour. He invited several American friends to dine with him in Chinatown, and the cook served chop suey. The Americans were delighted with the mixture of meat, vegetables, and sauce, and soon it was being served throughout the city. And why not? It was a great way to get rid of leftovers!

• ■ •

The ice cream cone was invented when an ice cream salesman ran out of bowls at the Louisiana Purchase Exposition in St. Louis in 1904. He bought waffles from a neighboring booth and rolled them into cones while he waited for the dishes to be washed. Customers liked the cones so much that he kept on using them.

• ■ •

The idea of describing an affront as "giving someone the cold shoulder" originated with food. In the Middle Ages, poor people who went to manors and castles, begging for food, were usually given the least-desirable leftover cut of meat—more often than not, a cold shoulder of mutton.

• ■ •

"Upsetting the apple cart" originally had nothing to do with a cart that hauled apples. (Apples were carried around in baskets.) Rather, the phrase came about in the 18th century and was used to describe kids who would pluck apples from trees, eat too many, and get sick.

• ■ •

It was 1930. He had all these little baking pans that he used to make strawberry shortcakes, only there were no orders for them. Instead, James Dewar used the pans to fill sponge cake with cream, thus inventing the Twinkie.

• ■ •

Milk is the food most commonly purchased in supermarkets, which is why it's usually placed toward the rear of the store; en route, customers often spot one or two more things they need and pick them up.

• ■ •

In the Middle Ages, eating humble pie was something people did, literally. The expression was originally "eating umbles pie," a meal consisting of the stringy or fatty remains of an animal (from the Latin *lumbulus*, or "loin"), usually a deer. People who ate it were poor and, thus, humble. By the 16th century, well-to-do people who had gotten too big for their jerkins were admonished to go out and eat some umbles pie.

• ■ •

On the other hand, "eating crow" was always synonymous with eating one's words. In Elizabethan England, it was common for one gentleman to disagree

with another by stating, "I've a crow to pluck with you."
When the argument was through, the loser would con-
sume the remains, figuratively speaking. (In the mid-
1800s, "crow-plucking" was replaced by "bone-pick-
ing," an expression inspired by dogs fighting over
bones.)

• ■ •

Legend has it that in 1617, King James I of England
enjoyed a cut of loin so much that he dubbed it Sir
Loin, hence the name. Other sources attribute the
name to the French *surlonge*, or "over the loin."
    We prefer the former. James was flaky enough to
have knighted beef . . . and it is, in any case, a much
better story.

• ▨ •

The graham cracker was invented by 19th-century
New England minister Sylvester Graham, who devised it to help fight alcoholism, promiscuity (which he
attributed to the consumption of red meat), and other
ills. He felt that the unsifted whole wheat flour used
in his crackers, in conjunction with a vegetarian diet,
would help to make people healthier and happier. And
you thought they just tasted good!
    Today, graham crackers comprise 15 percent of the
cracker market.
    Graham indirectly gave birth to the entire breakfast
cereal industry: among those who believed in what he
was doing was Dr. John Harvey Kellogg, who developed
Granose cereal and, later, corn flakes; one of Kellogg's

patients, Charles W. Post, came up with Elijah's Manna, which he later called Grape Nuts.

• ■ •

There really was a Dom Perignon, and he was the man who invented champagne. In the middle of the 17th century, the French monk sealed several bottles of wine with cork instead of oil-soaked cloth. The carbon dioxide produced by fermentation had nowhere to go, and the result was bubbly wine. Realizing he was on to something good, Dom produced more of the same, creating an important new business for the Champagne region.

• ■ •

The problem with turn-of-the-century candies was that they were often too big for a little child's mouth and too sticky to remove from the mouth. George Smith of Connecticut solved the problem in the early 1900s by creating the lollipop. It was named after Lolly Pop, a renowned racehorse of the day.

• ■ •

Pumpernickel bread got its name from Napoleon, or more accurately, from his horse. The dark bread that was served to the soldiers was scarce during the rough winter campaign in Russia, though Napoleon's horse, Nicoll, was always fed. The men grumbled among themselves that while they weren't eating, there was always enough *pain pour Nicholl* ("bread for Nicholl").

• ■ •

Chicken a la king was so-called in honor of King Edward VII, whose favorite recipe it was.

• ■ •

The flooding of rice paddies has very little to do with the nourishing of the rice. Farmers do it primarily to drown the weeds.

• ■ •

Parsley is put on plates for more than decoration. In the days before mints, people chewed it after a meal to freshen the breath.

Cheese was served before meals because, without knowing exactly why, cooks were aware that it helped kill the bacteria that cause tooth decay.

• ■ •

Jordan almonds have nothing to do with the nation or the river. The name is a corruption of the French word *jardin,* which means "garden."

• ■ •

The brand name Sanka, for decaffeinated coffee, is also derived from the French, from *sans cafeine* (sic). It was coined in 1903, shortly after the first decaffeinated coffee was created by accident. A shipment of coffee got wet during its journey from Europe to the U.S. When it was delivered to importer Dr. Ludwig Roselius, he found the beans still brewable, even though the resulting beverage had lost its kick.

• ■ •

The sweet-faced infant on the jars of Gerber baby food is not, as is popularly believed, a very young Humphrey Bogart. However, the original portrait was done by his mother, artist Maude Humphrey Bogart— hence, the misconception.

• ■ •

The carbonated beverage 7Up did not get its name from a game of craps or a lucky number seven or anything similar. Created in 1929, it was originally sold in seven-ounce containers. The "Up" part came from the direction in which the bubbles moved.

• ■ •

Eating celery causes you to lose weight: it burns more calories to eat it than the food itself contains. Licking a stamp is also a wash: the glue contains just under one-tenth of a calorie, which is about what you burn off moistening it.

In Israel, the glue is kosher.

• ■ •

Among the world's milk drinkers, 55 percent drink goat's milk and 45 percent drink cow's milk. The rest drink buffalo milk (Egypt and India), donkey and horse milk (China), camel milk (portions of Africa and Asia), and even yak and reindeer milk in Tibet and Lapland, respectively.

• ■ •

How did a baker's dozen come to mean 13 of something? Because of the way rolls, buns, and cakes were cooked in the 13th century, they were frequently sold in batches of a dozen. To prevent bakers from cheating their customers, London lawmakers passed laws which standardized the weight of these goods. To avoid stiff fines if the weight were off, bakers often threw in an extra item to make sure they made the required weight.

• ■ •

While we're on the subject of baked goods, soft, fluffy biscuits of today are not what they were in previous centuries. They were hard and dry, as the

French name implies (*bis* and *cuit* for "twice cooked"), baked so as to keep them fresh on long sea voyages.

• ■ •

Serving lemon with fish is a six hundred-year-old custom that has nothing to do with flavor. Rather, it was thought that if someone swallowed a bone, a mouthful of lemon juice would help to dissolve it. Ironically, there was some validity to the cure, though not for the reason people thought: sucking on a lemon caused the diner's throat muscles to contort, thus helping to free the bone.

• ■ •

Swiss cheese has holes, or "eyes," because of bacterial activity which occurs during fermentation. The bacteria produce gases which literally explode from the cheese, creating the eyes. Though Swiss cheese can be produced anywhere, the organisms and ingredients found in the mountains of Switzerland still produce the best cheese.

Geography

Although he discovered Australia and its surrounding land masses in 1642, only the island of Tasmania and the Tasman Sea were named after Dutch navigator Abel Janszoon Tasman.

Australia itself takes its name from the Latin *australis*, meaning "southern."

• ■ •

Angel Falls in Venezuela, the world's highest waterfall, was not so named because it seemed to pour from heaven. The truth is more mundane than that. It was named after Johnny Angel, the explorer who let the rest of us know it was there.

• ■ •

The infamous island off the coast of French Guiana is not called Devil's Island because of the heat. The name has to do with the murderous swells and whirlpools in the waters surrounding it.

• ■ •

The distance from the eastern side of Alaska to the western is nearly as great as the distance from New York to San Francisco.

• ■ •

Likewise, the eastern coast of Canada is closer to London than it is to its own western coast.

• ■ •

The only spot on earth from which you can see both the Atlantic and Pacific oceans is the summit of Mt. Izaru in Costa Rica.

• ■ •

Where on earth can you lose weight without dieting or exercise? On a mountaintop. You'll weigh even less if you climb to the top of a mountain near the equator. The gravitational pull of the earth decreases the farther you go from the center of the earth. Several miles above sea level, you'll weigh two or three pounds less than you do now (unless you're reading this on top of Mt. Everest, or in an airplane at cruising altitude which works just as well).

Likewise, because the earth bulges at the middle the equator is farther from the earth's center than the poles. Consequently, you'll weigh even less there.

None of this will help you get into your clothes any easier, though this is something ship companies have to keep in mind when planning how much fuel a vessel will need while plying the seas: just by sailing along the equator, for example, a twenty-thousand-ton ship can lose up to one-sixth of its weight!

• ■ •

Who decided that north should be at the top of a map?

It wasn't the Ancient Greeks or Romans. They put the east at the top of their maps, and that made sense: it was the direction of the rising sun. The early Christian and Moslem nations followed suit, since it was believed that the Garden of Eden had been located in the east, and east therefore deserved a place of honor on the map—just as it did in churches, where the altar was placed on the eastern side.

North gradually moved to the top of maps at the beginning of the 14th century because more and more armies, emissaries, and traders were traveling, and traveling north—that is, Europe—was where the bulk of the populated land areas were located.

• ■ •

In Greece, the farthest you can get from the sea is only 85 miles. And in England, it's just 65 miles.

• ■ •

The mouth of a river is called a delta because it resembles the triangular Greek letter of the same name.

• ■ •

Every language spoken today in Europe, North America, and most of the former Soviet Union, some six hundred million people in all, evolved from a single tongue. What is known as a "proto-Indo-European" language appears to have originated in what is now the southern Ukraine.

• ■ •

Though we're taught in school that there are seven continents, there are really only six, geographically speaking. The boundary between Europe and Asia is artificial, the work of ancient Greek mapmakers who believed the two regions were separated almost entirely by water from the Aegean to the North Sea. When the truth became known, it wasn't enough to displace tradition . . . or European resistance to the idea of being considered part of Asia.

• ■ •

Most everyone knows that Chicago is the Windy City, though not many people know why it's called this. In 1893, the World's Columbian Exposition was held in Chicago, celebrating the daring of Christopher Columbus. So bombastic was the city's praise for the fair and for itself that the New York press (never inclined to be charitable to the "second city") took to calling Chicago the Windy City.

• ■ •

The Black Sea isn't made of black water, of course: the black color of the water comes from decomposition of vegetation caused by bacteria that live in the landlocked body. The sea also happens to be rough, gloomy, and thickly fogged, which is why it was originally called *Pontus Euxinus* ("inhospitable sea") by the Greeks.

The Red Sea got its name from the reddish algae that live in the waters.

• ■ •

When Los Angeles was founded by Felipe de Neve in 1781, its full name was El Pueblo de Nuestra Señora La Reina de Los Angeles—The Town of Our Lady the Queen of the Angels.

• ■ •

The Pacific Ocean covers more area than all the land on earth combined. And at 64 million square miles, it's twice as large as the Atlantic Ocean.

• ■ •

The largest city in the U.S. isn't New York or even Los Angeles, it's Juneau, Alaska. The city covers 3,108 square miles, making it seven times larger than L.A. The largest city in the contiguous 48 states is Jacksonville, Florida, which is 460 square miles—twice the size of L.A.

The most populous city continues to be New York, followed by L.A. and Chicago. (New York's held the title for quite some time, in fact; in 1790, the first census revealed that the most populous cities were New York, Philadelphia, and Baltimore, in that order.)

• ■ •

With the exception of Antarctica, all of the Earth's continents are wider in the northern section than in the southern section. Scientists cannot account for this phenomenon.

• ■ •

Mt. Everest may be the world's highest mountain, but it's not the tallest. At 33,476 feet, Mauna Kea on the island of Hawaii is some four thousand feet taller. However, the mountain's huge base is submerged, allowing Everest to rise higher from sea level.

Actually, the jury is still out on whether Everest is even the highest. Recent satellite measurements place Everest at 29,028 feet and its fellow Himalyayan peak, K-2, at 29,030 feet. Snow cover, erosion, and the fact that the mountains are still being pushed skyward make exact measurement difficult.

In any case, 96 of the world's 109 tallest peaks are located in the Himalayas.

• ■ •

Though "Podunk" is a pejorative term for a small, isolated town, there is no town actually called by that name. The Podunks were Indians who lived in South Windsor, Connecticut, at the mouth of a stream which still bears the name. The Indians disappeared without a trace in 1676 (apparently they joined another tribe), and finding the Podunks became something of a local joke. By the early 18th century, New Englanders were using it to describe any place that was too remote, lost, or small to locate.

Along similar lines, insignificant towns are called "Jerkwater" because their only perceived purpose was for providing water to trains passing through. This was done by cranking the water from tanks, or "jerking water."

At soda fountains, this process is also called jerking.

Health and Fitness

Forget what your mother used to tell you! It's actually safer to go swimming on a full stomach than on an empty one. Cramps aren't caused by food in the belly but by cold water and muscle exhaustion. Food provides fuel for the body, and the digestive process raises the body's temperature.

The problem that should concern moms is *overeating*, which can lead to sleepiness and dulled reflexes.

• ■ •

Pirates didn't wear earrings for decoration, but for their health and well-being. There are pressure points just above the earlobe, points which, according to today's acupuncturists, help to improve eyesight, reduce the appetite, and boost energy levels—qualities which came in handy on the high seas.

Some of the earrings also had waxy lumps dangling from the bottom, which helped the pirates in another way: during exchanges of cannon fire, they were used to plug the ears.

• ■ •

The modern condom was invented by a gentleman of that name (or something close to it; no one is sure), who devised it for England's King Charles II in the middle of the 17th century. Charles was concerned about bastard children and venereal disease, both of which the inventor's lamb intestine sheath was designed to prevent.

There are records of earlier, less effective condoms made in ancient China using lubricated silk paper. The ancient Romans are said to have experimented with condoms made of the muscles of fallen foes.

• ■ •

The earliest known form of birth control was devised in Egypt in 2000 B.C. and consisted of crocodile excrement (to prevent the semen from penetrating) and honey (to prevent the odor from repelling suitors).

• ■ •

Why do the astrological Cancer the Crab and the disease have the same name? *Cancer* means "crab" in Greek, and the veins around cancerous growths tend to be distended, suggesting the legs of a crab to the Greeks.

• ■ •

Despite the way it's portrayed in *Ben-Hur*, leprosy is not a disease that causes people to fall apart, nor is it even moderately communicable. It's caused by an organism, and results in ulcerations and a deadening of nerves. In its most serious cases, leprosy may result in infection that costs the sufferer a finger or toe. More often than not, the loss of sensation in the extremities is what causes victims to lose them in accidents with fire, tools, etc.

• ■ •

Time-release capsules work by virtue of a digestible waxlike coating applied to each pellet. The thicker the coating, the longer it takes for the medicine inside to be released.

• ■ •

No, people never believed that chicken pox came from chickens. In Old English it was known as *gican*, ("itching") pox. Something was lost in the translation.

Home and Hearth

Why do we use piggy banks and not, for example, bunny banks?

In medieval England, clay was known as *pygg*, and people would put their coins in *pygg* dishes or jars when they came home. One English potter, circa 1600, was asked to make a *pygg* bank; unfamiliar with the term or the dishes, he made several banks shaped like pigs, with slots in the back. The charming idea caught on and quickly spread throughout Europe.

• ■ •

Dinner knives (as opposed to steak knives) lost their points in 1669, when Cardinal Richelieu of France became disgusted with people who used them to pick their teeth. However, those close to the Cardinal suspected that he had the knife points rounded to discourage assassination attempts. Rulers and lords throughout Europe saw the wisdom in what he'd done and soon followed suit.

• ■ •

Barns are not painted red so that animals can find their way back to them. (Many farm animals are color-blind.) The least expensive paint has always been white, but rather than simply whitewash barns, farmers would mix in pigments found in the earth—most of which were red.

•   ■   •

Who decided that lawns, rather than easier-to-maintain rock gardens or wood chips, should surround our homes? It was an outgrowth, so to speak, of the popularity of lawn bowling and golf in early 19th-century England. Not just the nobility, but even the owners of small cottages enjoyed the sports. The games caught on here and, as a result, so did well-manicured lawns.

The Human Body

Coffee does not help a person sober up. At best, the time spent drinking it allows the body to burn off the alcohol, at a rate of approximately one-half ounce an hour.

• ■ •

No, dreams aren't over in just a few seconds. You experience them in real time, and the average dream lasts approximately twenty minutes. Most people have four to six dreams each night.

• ■ •

Most classical Greek statues, paintings of beauties or hunks, and even Marilyn Monroe, had second toes that are longer than all the others. Why this suggests sex appeal is not known; only 15 percent of people have this variation.

Moving a bit higher—

• ■ •

—On most human hands, the middle finger is exactly as long as the hand is wide.

• ■ •

There are two reasons people react negatively to screeching chalk and other high-pitched sounds. First, the ear tends to amplify higher sounds, making them louder than they actually are, so we can hear them easily. Second, like tickling, the element of surprise makes these sounds seem even worse than they are. Combined, the qualities make shrill noises unpleasant to some and unbearable to others.

• ■ •

When pregnant women eat pickles, it isn't the pickle they crave, per se. It's the salt, which is a key ingredient in the amniotic fluid and also helps the mother produce the extra blood she needs to nurture the fetus.

If a pickle isn't available, pretzels or an anchovy pizza will work just as well.

• ■ •

Yawning is not contagious. The act itself helps bring air into the lungs and blood to the brain. When several people yawn at the same time, they're simply responding to the same stimuli—stuffy atmosphere or boredom—not someone else's yawn.

• ■ •

Most people believe that when a limb "falls asleep," it's because the flow of blood has been interrupted.

Not so. The condition is called neurapraxia, and it happens when a nerve is compressed between a bone and another relatively hard object such as a chair, mattress, crossed legs, etc.

If the blood supply were cut off for a night, the limb would not be asleep in the morning; it would be dead.

• ■ •

There's no such thing as a double-joint. A "double-jointed" person is simply one with looser ligaments than the rest of us.

• ■ •

Strange as it may seem, the reason a scratch stops an itch is because you're hurting yourself. An itch is an irritation of the nerve endings close to the surface of the skin; scratching causes a pain which overrides the itching. If scratching has removed an external cause of the itch—dust or a loose thread, for example—it won't return. If the cause is internal—a mosquito bite or allergic reaction—the itch most likely will return.

• ■ •

Pain travels 350 feet in a second, and involves roughly ten billion nerve cells per square inch of skin. Pain moves quicker than your ability to react to it, which is why you usually get your palm burned before you remove it from a hot surface.

• ■ •

Bad breath can't always be treated by mouthwash. Certain foods, like onions, have oils which go from the stomach, to the bloodstream, to the lungs, and stay there for hours, where all the mouthwash in the world won't get rid of it.

• ■ •

It's now believed that one reason humans began to walk upright is so they could remain relatively cool during the hot midday hours: the more erect the human, the less skin surface is exposed to the rising sun.

• ■ •

More of the body's weight comes from muscle than from bone: the average adult male has 40 pounds of bone compared to just over 65 pounds of muscle. The average adult female has 15 percent less.

• ■ •

Of the 206 bones in the human body, one-quarter of them are located in the feet.

• ■ •

No matter how dry your mouth may feel, the sensation of thirst arises in the pharynx, the part of the body that connects the mouth and nasal passages with the esophagus. As our blood loses moisture, the cells of the pharynx become especially tight and dry, signaling us that it's time for a drink.

• ■ •

Exercise causes us to become especially thirsty not only because we perspire and lose water, but also because we breathe through the mouth, causing additional drying of the pharynx. That's why we're still thirsty even after bloating our stomachs with water or Gatorade.

• ■ •

The face turns white with fright (as do the hands and feet, though no one ever bothers to check) because the body marshals its blood supplies to fuel the heart and organs with the extra energy needed to run or fight.

A blush is just the opposite, nature's way of signaling

a potential sexual partner that they've warmed us and we have no intention of running.

• ■ •

When we lose warmth from our extremities due to fear or cold, tiny muscles contract, making the skin tighten and forcing the hair to stand up, giving us goose bumps. This is a largely vestigial process, which worked a lot better when we had more hair on our bodies, and the hair's stiffening was a means of trapping air against the skin and keeping us warm.

• ■ •

What exactly does 20/20 vision mean? It means that at 20 feet you can read letters on an eye chart that a person with perfect vision should be able to read at 20 feet. If you have 20/30 vision, you can read letters at 20 feet that a person with normal vision would be able to read at 30 feet, and so on.

• ■ •

The reason dim objects such as stars look brighter when we view them from the side of the eye instead of directly, is simple. Our eyes are filled with rods and cones. The color-sensitive cones are located in the middle of the eye and are most active during the day. The rods are much more sensitive to light, and are collected around the sides of the eye; to access them directly, it's necessary to look at an object indirectly.

• ■ •

Déjà vu—the distinct feeling that you've been some-where or seen something before—is nothing more exotic than crossed wires. An image is flashed to your brain and recorded in memory an instant before it heads over to awareness. Though scientists know this happens, they aren't sure why.

• ■ •

Talk about taking the long way around: blood has to go through your entire body in order to get from one side of the heart to the other.

• ■ •

Your skin wrinkles when you sit in a bathtub because it's expanding. As you soak, the epidermis absorbs water, causing it to bulge. You notice it only on the hands and feet, though, because the skin there is rela-tively hard and rough and it expands less uniformly than in other, more pliable sections of the body.

• ■ •

How is it possible for a person to blow hot and cold simply by changing the shape of the mouth?
   Hold your wrist six inches from your mouth. If you blow forcefully, with your lips tight, the relatively in-tense heat of your breath causes the moisture on your

skin to evaporate, creating a *sensation* of coolness. If you move your wrist right up to your mouth, there isn't time for air around your wrist to cool and it feels hot.

Likewise, if you blow gently on your wrist, with your mouth wide, the heat isn't sufficient to affect the moistures.

• ■ •

Hair doesn't turn gray or white as we age; it turns translucent. Hair only appears to be gray or white because the follicles stop manufacturing pigment, allowing light to appear increasingly white as it passes through the hair.

The loss of pigment is also what causes skin to become blotchy with age.

Insects and Arachnids

If you go outside during the summer, around dusk, chances are good gnats will circle your head. The reason is that they are drawn to moisture—specifically, the kind with nutrients that appeal to them; those contained in tears, perspiration, and blood. If you're absolutely determined to stay outside, a big gash on your arm will draw the gnats from your face.

• ■ •

Earthworms breathe through their skin, which is why they're found on sidewalks and paths after it rains. If they didn't leave the soil, they'd drown.

Worms also leave the earth in the morning, when the sun has not yet evaporated the moisture that collects there; that's when the early bird usually gets them.

• ■ •

Here's something you may not want to contemplate: the largest insect in the world is the atlas moth, which has a ten-inch wingspan. The heaviest insect is the goliath beetle, which weighs one-quarter of a pound.

Be glad you don't live in the days of the dinosaur, when dragonflies had a wingspan of up to two feet.

• ■ •

You will never find a female firefly. Ladies of the species are called glowworms, and their light is half as bright as that of the males. Only the males fly.

• ■ •

Mexican jumping beans jump because there's a bean moth larva inside. The egg is laid in the flower of the bean, which closes around it as it grows. While the larva matures, it feeds on the bean, eventually gnawing its way out. When the little worm wriggles, the bean moves.

• ■ •

Don't blame them all: of the 112,000 species of butterfly and moth, only three species of moth eat wool clothing or carpet, and then almost always in the larval stage. Not surprisingly, they're known as clothes moths.

• ■ •

Termites don't really eat wood. Oh, they ingest it, all right. But the digesting is left to microscopic life forms that live in their intestines and eat the cellulose in wood. When that's been removed, the other ingredients in the wood are left for the termite to metabolize.

• ■ •

Flies are able to walk on walls and ceilings thanks to tiny pincers at the end of each of their six legs. These allow flies to hold on while they secure their position with suctionlike pads between the claws.

• ■ •

If you can't seem to swat the fly that's infiltrated your house, don't worry: the life span of a housefly is just two weeks. If you do decide to hunt it down, though, use a fly swatter instead of your hand, a magazine, or a towel. Flies are covered with hairs that sense changes in the air; with its hole-riddled surface, a fly-swatter creates a negligible disturbance compared to those made by a solid object.

• ■ •

Webs produced by outdoor and indoor spiders are both composed of liquid secretions which harden on contact with the air. What turns webs into "cobwebs" is simply the fact that dust collects on them. Until then, they usually aren't even noticed.

The weight of the collected dust often tears the corners of the cobwebs down, giving them that mossy, hanging appearance familiar in horror films.

Cob, incidentally, is an Old English word for spider.

Inventors and Inventions

You can thank the 17th-century Belgian engineer Jacques de Liege for putting the "jack" in the "jackknife" he invented. Before then, knives didn't fold.

• ■ •

Also in Belgium, the 19th-century inventor Antoine Sax gave us the saxophone. Meanwhile, in nearby France . . .

• ■ •

. . . the silhouette got its name from the 18th-century finance minister Etienne de Silhouette, who was extraordinarily skilled at cutting peoples' likenesses from black paper.

• ■ •

Do gun silencers really work as well as they do in the movies? Sometimes.

The explosive blast that comes from firing a bullet can only be silenced when the gasses are released from the rear. (That leaves out revolvers, which emit them from the side.) The silencer grabs the gas and, by means of strands of steel or bronze wool, quickly breaks it down, cooling it and letting it go slowly and more quietly. There's still a "pop," but it's less than a quarter as loud as the gunfire itself.

The silencer was invented by Hiram Percy Maxim, who also created the car muffler.

• ■ •

In 1827, British chemist John Walker forgot about a stirring stick he left in a beaker of antimony and potash. When he tried to rub the mixture off, it burst into flame, and the match was invented.

• ■ •

In 1926, 3M began producing tapes to mask automobiles, or "scotch" off certain portions, so manufacturers could paint straight lines. However, the manufacturer used a relatively inexpensive adhesive that leaked, making it unusable.

What to do with the tons of leftovers? 3M decided to sell it to the general public, packaged it with a tartan design, and called it Scotch tape.

• ■ •

The Wright Brothers' original plane flew just once,
on December 17, 1903. Not long after the 12-sec-
ond flight ended, the wind upended the plane and
smashed it. The brothers took the pieces home to Day-
ton from Kitty Hawk, N.C., and built more aerody-
namic models based on what they learned.

Today, the plane, in one piece, is on display at the
Smithsonian's Air and Space Museum.

• ■ •

Charles Rolls, co-founder of Rolls-Royce, was the first
man to fly both ways across the English Channel.
That's the good news. The bad news is, he was also
the first man to die in a plane crash in England when
his Wright Brothers–built biplane went down from a
height of fifty feet.

• ■ •

Sunglasses were invented by the Chinese in the 13th
century, and were used by judges so that accused
persons couldn't "read" their eyes. Sunglasses were first
used in the 20th century by the Army Air Corps which,
in 1932, created glasses that would help alleviate the
glare encountered by pilots.

• ■ •

In August, 1907, aware of the slowness of the U.S. Postal Service, teenagers Jim Casey and Claude Ryan established the American Messenger Company in Seattle. The company was successful, and several years later changed its name to the United Parcel Service.

• ■ •

The self-inflating airbag—essentially the same kind that is used today in automobiles—was first patented in 1849 by an Illinois attorney, who designed it to raise boats off shoals. But the inventor was preoccupied with his caseload and a burgeoning interest in politics, so it remained for someone other than Abraham Lincoln to do something with the invention.

• ■ •

Alexander Graham Bell invented the telephone in 1876, but it's a little known fact that his assistant Watson—who was the recipient of the first phone message—"Mr. Watson, come here, I want you"—was the inventor of the telephone booth.

• ■ •

There was no "1" on old telephone dials due to electronics. Each time a caller turned the dial, it clicked (you can still hear this on "pulse-tone" settings). Any number of things could have sent a one-click signal, which the phone would have misinterpreted as a "1." Thus, dials started with "2".

Today, of course, "1" doesn't present a problem and is used for toll calling.

• ■ •

We've also done away with the original greeting used on telephones. When regular phone service was first inaugurated, in New Haven, CT, in 1878, people said, "Ahoy," instead of "Hello." New Haven is located on the busy Long Island Sound, which accounts for the nautical greeting.

• ■ •

The first telephone directory, issued that same year in New Haven, contained just fifty names. There were no numbers. You simply called the operator ("Ahoy!") and asked for the individual you wanted to talk to.

• ■ •

Manholes are round rather than square or rectangular so that they can't fall through the opening when being removed. A lip inside the hole prevents the circular cover from fitting through no matter how it's turned or moved.

• ■ •

Albert Einstein left school at the age of fifteen, but Thomas Edison did him one better: he entered school at the age of eight and left after three months, when his teacher described him as "addled." Edison's mother taught him at home and he went on to patent more inventions, 1,093, than anyone else.

• ■ •

The first words ever recorded on Edison's "speaking machine" was "Mary had a little lamb." It's not Patrick Henry, but it does have a certain charm. . . .

• ■ •

Edison also invented the incandescent light in 1879. It took just three years before entrepreneurs were using his creation to save lives, replacing dangerous candles with strings of Christmas lights.

• ■ •

It figures: Edison proposed to his future wife, Mina Miller, using Morse code. They'd known each other a year before he mustered the nerve to tap out, "Will you marry me?" She tapped back, "Yes."

• ■ •

The Bic pen got its name in 1938, from the French entrepreneur Baron Biche, whose firm produced the original ballpoint pens for Hungarian inventor Laszlo Biro.

• ■ •

The monkey wrench got its name due to a mistranslation. It was invented by Charles Moncke of London, and when it came to the U.S. it was called by the way the name sounded, not by the way it was written.

Landmarks

London's Big Ben isn't the clock or the tower of England's Houses of Parliament. It's the 13.5-ton bell. Cast in 1858, it was named after Sir Benjamin Hall, who was Commissioner of Works when the bell was installed.

• ■ •

Charlotte Bartholdi, the mother of designer Frédéric Auguste Bartholdi, was the model for the face of the Statue of Liberty; his girlfriend Jeanne-Emilie was the model for the statue's arms. Alexandre Gustave Eiffel, who built the Eiffel Tower, built the metal skeleton.

• ■ •

Baltimore's Johns Hopkins University is not named after two people; the founder's first name was really Johns, thanks to an eccentric family tradition.

• ■ •

The famous Holland Tunnel, which connects New York and New Jersey under the Hudson River, was not named for the nationality of the original Manhattan colonists. It was named after Clifford Milburn Holland, the engineer who directed the tunnel-building operation from 1910–1924. The tunnel was finished three years after Holland's death.

Language

The interesting and oft-told origin of the word "tip" as a gratuity to a waiter is, alas, apocryphal. There is no evidence that boxes in English inns and pubs, used to hold coins to "tip" the waiters, ever bore the words "to insure promptness." The English would have bristled over such obvious extortion.

Rather, the word comes from the 16th-century verb "tip," which meant to give unexpectedly. It was derived from the German word *tippen*, which means "to tap."

• ■ •

The phrase "kick the bucket" originally connoted a suicide. In medieval times, suicide victims usually tied a rope to their neck, slung it over a rafter, then leapt off a bucket. Most kicked it as they strangled and convulsed.

• ■ •

The word "boycott" comes from Captain Charles Cunningham Boycott (1832–1897), who worked for Lord Erne in Connemara, Ireland. He was a hard-hearted rent collector, and eventually Erne's tenants got together and refused to work or to pay. Their methods were successful and spread to other estates, and the word has stayed with us.

• ■ •

Down the road a bit, in Ballyhooly, Cork, the propensity of the villagers to fight and yell and call attention to themselves gave birth to the word "ballyhoo."

• ■ •

The expression "Curiosity killed the cat" does not refer directly to a feline. First used in the 18th century, the expression refers to local gossips who poke, pry, and backbite like cats.

The phrase which it apparently parodied, "Care will kill a cat," appears in George Wither's 17th-century poem *Christmas*, and suggests that a cat who is *not* curious will lose its nine lives to boredom.

• ■ •

Why is the phrase "rhyme nor reason" used to describe something that makes no sense? Reading something incomprehensible that a friend had written, Sir Thomas More suggested he turn it into verse. The friend did and, after reading it, More said, "That's better! It's rhyme now, anyway. Before, it was neither rhyme nor reason."

• ■ •

The expression "right away," meaning "immediately," comes from the earliest railroad cries for "right of way," meaning get your wagon, handcart, or cow off the track pronto.

• ■ •

Having the dickens scared out of you has nothing to do with Charles. It's an expression the English borrowed from the German *decken*, "to cover." In other words, it's something that scares the coverings off us, causing us to run.

• ■ •

Until the end of the 15th century, punctuation was virtually nonexistent; only spaces between words and sentences indicated when one ended and another began. The Italian scholar and printer Aldus Manutius is credited with having invented modern punctuation by using dots and other markings.

• ■ •

How did "talking turkey" come to mean being honest? According to records in the Library of Congress, in 1848, when a U.S. engineer and an Indian were deciding which bird to eat, the white man said, "You can have the buzzard and I will take the turkey, or I will take the turkey and you can have the buzzard."

Hearing this, the Indian said, "Why don't you talk turkey with me?"

Those who overheard the conversation began using the expression out west and made it part of the language.

• ■ •

Though the term "late," as applied to the recently dead, covers a period of about twenty years, it can also be used if the life of the dead person overlapped that of the person using the term. To many people, JFK is still a "late" president.

The word may seem odd to use in connection with the dead, though not when you consider the source: it was first used in reference to medieval rulers who went by only one name. To avoid confusion between dead Peters, Philipses, or Charleses, the speaker would say, "Charles, late the King of England."

• ■ •

"Paying through the nose" was not originally intended to mean paying until it hurts, but paying an unjust amount. It comes from the 16th-century Swedes, who counted the noses in a region and assessed a tax accordingly. Large families with low income paid more than small families with large income, which was deemed unfair, i.e., paying through the nose.

• ■ •

There are no English words that rhyme with "orange," "purple," or "silver." None.

• ■ •

And the only two words that end in "gry" are "angry" and "hungry." The word "gry" itself, once a unit of measure meant equal to .008 of an inch, is no longer used. Only three words end in "ceed": "exceed," "proceed," and "succeed," while only four words end in "efy": "liquefy," "putrefy," "rarefy," and "stupefy."

• ■ •

The word "queue" is the only English word that's pronounced the same with or without its last four letters.

• ■ •

Winning something "hands down" did not come from placing a winning card hand facedown. It comes from the early days of horse racing. If a horse was well ahead of the pack, the jockey would release the reins and put his "hands down" on the horse, giving the animal free-rein ... and the language another expression.

• ■ •

If there's blackmail, is there also whitemail? You bet. In 16th-century England, "mail" meant rent or tribute. Whitemail was a debt paid in silver; blackmail was a debt paid in any other medium, from grain to meat. Whitemail had a set value; blackmail did not, allowing the one to whom it was owed to extort more than the actual debt.

• ■ •

The term "red herring," meaning something misleading, comes from the use of herring—which becomes red when smoked—to train dogs to follow a scent. Unfortunately, escaped prisoners would try to get hold of red herrings to toss here and there to distract the dogs set after them, hence the expression.

• ■ •

The buck that President Truman said "stops here" had nothing to do with money. He was referring to a knife with a buckhorn handle. Card players would move the dagger around the table as a way to keep track of whose deal it was.

"Buck," signifying money, comes from buckskins, which trappers would use as payment in lieu of currency.

• ■ •

Before it was a joint in the hand, the word "knuckle" meant the knee joint, from which we get the expression "knuckle under." The word derives from the German *knochen*, or "bone."

"Knucklehead," as a term of derision, also comes from German, meaning the skull (and what's inside it) is solid bone.

• ■ •

The phrase "in cold blood" never had anything to do with the temperature of the blood of the victim. Rather, it always described a crime planned and committed mercilessly ... unlike a hotblooded crime, which is committed in the passion of the moment.

• ■ •

In 17th- and 18th-century England, wealthy men were robbed by thugs who first tugged their wool wigs down so they couldn't see. From this we get the expression "pulling the wool over one's eyes."

• ■ •

The longest single-word palindromes are "redivider" and "releveler."

• ■ •

The use of the words "red tape" to describe bureau-cracy comes from the centuries-old English practice of sealing important documents with red tape and a red wax seal. Cutting through a lot of it was the only way to get to the bottom of governmental matters.

• ■ •

Finding oneself between the devil and the deep blue sea has nothing to do with Lucifer. Rather, a "devil" is a seam in a wooden ship's hull, lying just at the waterline. It was nicknamed the devil because, when it sprung a leak, it was extremely difficult to reach from the inside. Thus, repairs were usually done outside where, depending on swells, there was usually just a narrow space between the devil and the deep blue sea.

• ■ •

One of the Holy Grails of etymology is the true ori-gina of the word "ok." Some etymologists ascribe it to Andrew Jackson's misspelling of "all correct" as "oll kurrect"; others to Martin Van Buren's birthplace Old Kinderhook; others to the Jamaican *oh ki* for "all right." There are other possible sources, including German, Dutch, Scottish, and African phrases, but the truth is, no one knows.

• ■ •

Siamese twins are so called after Chang and Eng, a pair born in Siam in 1811. Ironically, their father was Chinese and their mother was half-Chinese making them only one-quarter Siamese. Their names not surprisingly, meant "right" and "left," respectively.

• ■ •

An expression for drunkenness, "three sheets to (or "in") the wind," originated in the late 18th century among sailors. A sheet is not a sail, as one might suppose, but a rope or chain attached to a sail to set its angle. If the sheets are loose, the ship will move willy-nilly through the seas, like a drunken sailor through the streets of a port city.

Etymologists aren't certain whether the "wind" refers to the sea breeze or is short for the windlass.

• ■ •

The phrase "son of a gun" also originated on ships in the early 18th century, when women were allowed to accompany their husbands or newfound boyfriends on long sea voyages. During such voyages, mothers gave birth to their children behind a canvas curtain near the midship gun. If the paternity of the newborn was in doubt—and often it was, as many of the women had been prostitutes—the child was somewhat face-tiously registered in the log as the "son of a gun."

• ■ •

The phrase "no love lost between them" is a corruption of both the wording and intention of the author. Taken from the anonymous ballad "The Babes in the Wood," the original statement goes, "No love between this two was lost/Each was to other kind/In love they lived, in love they died/And left two babes behind."

In other words, the subjects loved each other deeply. Who changed it and why is not known.

• ■ •

Contrary to popular misconception, the longest English word is not "antidisestablishmentarianism." Nor is it "floccinaucinihilipilificationism." No, the longest word is "pneumonoultramicroscopicsilicovolcanoconiosis," which describes a lung disease caused by breathing in particles of volcanic matter or a smiliar fine dust.

An even longer word, one hundred letters long, was used by James Joyce in *Finnegans Wake* (1939), created to describe a thunderclap at the beginning of the story: "bababadalgharaghtakamminarronnkonnbronnt-onnerronntuonnthunntrovarrhounawnskawntoohooho-ordenenthurnuk."

For the record, the longest word Shakespeare ever used was "honorificabilitudinitatibus." It's in *Love's Labour's Lost* (1594).

• ■ •

The term "sadist," of course, is derived from the name of the Marquis de Sade, a French soldier and novelist who specialized in sexual abuse (and spent a total of twenty-seven years in prison for his offenses). However, the term "masochist" also derives from an infamous historical figure: Leopold von Sacher-Masoch, a 19th-century German novelist whose works depicted various forms of sexual self-abuse.

• ■ •

The sentence "Jackdaws love my big sphinx of quartz" is the shortest sentence ever created which contains all the letters of the alphabet. If you want to try your hand at a shorter one, these are the only extra letters in the sentence: a, i, o, and s.

• ■ •

"Aspirin" is something of an anagram. The "a" comes from the first letter of acetylsalicylic acid, the scientific term for the drug. The "spir" is from *Spiraea ulmaria*, a plant used in its manufacture. And the "in" was a suffix typically applied to chemical and mineralogical goods (such as glycerin and acetin).

• ■ •

Of all the states in the U.S., Maine is the only one with a single-syllable name.

• ■ •

The expression "Hip! Hip! Hurrah!" was originally used to taunt Jews. In Germany of the Middle Ages, the word was "Hep," an anagram for *Hierosolyma est perdita*, "Jerusalem is destroyed." The Eastern Europeans added *huraj*, "To paradise!", which is where they thought they were headed, and the expression took its modern form and meaning.

• ■ •

"Tell it to the marines!" originated with King Charles II of England. When told that certain sailors had seen flying fish and other amazing sights during a lengthy voyage to the east, he decreed that no events should ever be dismissed until they were first told to the marines, who had apparently seen everything.

The Law

Marijuana wasn't illegal until 1937. Prior to that, the government wasn't sure it had the right to outlaw a plant. It was finally banned in a roundabout way: Congress said you couldn't sell it without a license, then declined to issue any licenses. It wasn't until 1970 that the government banned marijuana outright.

• ■ •

It has never been against the law for buyers to remove those infamous tags from their mattresses. The warning, "Not to be removed under penalty of law" applies to the seller. Once you buy it, you can do whatever you want to it.

• ■ •

Al Capone was one of the most notorious gang leaders of the 20th century, but what did his oldest brother Vincent do for a living? He was a police officer in Nebraska. He is on record as having disapproved of his brother's activities, which included bootlegging, extortion, murder, and tax evasion.

• ■ •

The first copyright law wasn't passed until England enacted one in 1709. Prior to that, publication of a work implicitly constituted ownership, though this was extremely difficult to enforce because so many plays, songs, and poems were written and performed but not printed.

• ■ •

The Supreme Court's 1966 Miranda ruling, which required police to inform crime suspects of their rights, did not help Ernesto Miranda: though he was retried after the ruling, he was re-convicted and was sent to jail. He was eventually freed, then murdered in 1976 when a fight broke out during a card game.

Literature

In the original tale, Cinderella's slipper was made of fur, not glass. The story was passed along orally for centuries; when Charles Perrault finally wrote it down in 1697, he mistook *vair,* ("ermine,") for verre, ("glass"). He later realized his mistake, but the story was so popular he elected not to change it.

• ■ •

When Hamlet adjures Ophelia, "Get thee to a nunnery," he's not referring to a place where nuns dwell. He's telling his girlfriend to go to a brothel. Obviously, he was not showing concern for the lass but was making a cynical statement about her overt advances.

• ■ •

Speaking of *Hamlet,* no one in the play says, "Methinks the lady doth protest too much." What Gertrude says is, "The lady protests too much, methinks." In any case, what Gertrude means is that the lady "proclaims" too much, not "complains." This gives the phrase rather a different meaning.

• ■ •

And no one in *Hamlet* said, "There's a method to his madness." Not exactly, anyway. Polonius says of Hamlet's apparent pscyhosis, "Though this be madness, yet there is method in't."

• ■ •

Before leaving *Hamlet*, we should point out that the play is Shakespeare's longest: at 3,931 lines, it's nearly twice as long as his shortest, *Macbeth*, which runs 2,108 lines . . . and *still* takes a good three hours to perform!

• ■ •

Daniel Defoe's *Robinson Crusoe* was inspired by the true-life story of Scottish sailor Alexander Selkirk, who lived on an uninhabited Caribbean island for 52 months, from 1704–1709, before he was rescued.

• ■ •

In case you're holding a transfer, the other streetcar in Tennessee Williams' *A Streetcar Named Desire* (1947) is named Cemetery. Not surprisingly, they share the same track.

• ■ •

In the original 1904 edition of *Peter Pan*, the hero takes the Darling children to Neverland, not Never-Never Land. The latter gained notoriety through the animated Disney film and Mary Martin musical, both in the early 1950s.

• ■ •

Yes, the Library of Congress stocks erotic fiction, including examples of modern pornography. The works are in a separate collection, and you have to be over eighteen to request the books.

• ■ •

The detective story was invented by horror writer Edgar Allan Poe. His amateur sleuth, C. Auguste Dupin, was featured in the short stories "The Murders in the Rue Morgue," "The Mystery of Marie Roget," and "The Purloined Letter" in the 1840s. The stories established the tone and format followed by writers from Sir Arthur Conan Doyle to Dashiell Hammett. The annual Mystery Writers of America award is named the Edgar in Poe's honor.

• ■ •

Speaking of detectives, in none of the Sherlock Holmes stories does the sleuth say, "Elementary, my dear Watson," to his friend. He does say "elementary" once, in "The Crooked Man" (1894), but that's it. It

was the movies that put those words in Sherlock's
mouth.

•	■	•

The science fiction story was not the invention of
Jules Verne or H.G. Wells, but of Lucian of Samo-
sata, who lived from 125–200 A.D. In his *The True
History*, the Greek author writes about a trip to the
moon.

•	■	•

The dolls in author Jacqueline Susann's *Valley of the
Dolls* (1966) aren't women and they aren't toys.
They're the pills consumed by actresses in the novel.
  Valley of the Dolls has sold in excess of 24 million
copies, making it the top-selling novel of all time. *The
Godfather* is number two, at 15 million copies.

•	■	•

It was a match made in a graveyard: Washington Irving, the author of *The Legend of Sleepy Hollow*, was
passionately in love with Mary Shelley, the author of
Frankenstein. They met when Irving lived in France
from 1824–1826. Shelley, who was 27 years old at the
time and 14 years his junior, had been widowed for
two years.
  The romance ended when Irving returned to the
U.S.; Shelley opted not to return with him, and broke
his heart.

• ■ •

In 1936, author Margaret Mitchell's original title for her one and only novel was *Tomorrow is Another Day*. However, her publisher felt there were too many novels with "tomorrow" in their title so she came up with another name: *Gone With the Wind*. The title came from Ernest Dowson's 19th-century poem "Cynara."

Likewise, Scarlett O'Hara was going to be called Pansy until Ms. Mitchell changed her mind.

• ■ •

The title of Ken Kesey's novel *One Flew Over the Cuckoo's Nest* (1962) is from an old nursery rhyme:
  Wire, briar, limber, lock,
  Three geese in a flock,
  One flew East, one flew West,
  One flew over the cuckoo's nest.

• ■ •

Before writing the novel *Jaws* (1974), author Peter Benchley wrote speeches for President Lyndon Johnson.

• ■ •

The surname of poet Edna St. Vincent Millay is just Millay; St. Vincent is her middle name. It came from the name of the hospital in Rockford, Maine,

where her mother had a pleasant stay when the future
poet was born.

• ■ •

"To err is human, to forgive divine," is not from the
Bible, as many people think. It's from Alexander
Pope's *Essay on Criticism* (1711). Likewise, "A jug of
wine, a loaf of bread—and thou," oft-misconstrued as
Biblical, is from Iranian poet Omar Khayyám's 12th-
century *Robā'īyāt*.

• ■ •

The opening lines of Longfellow's 1839 poem "The
Village Blacksmith" are among the most misunder-
stood in American poetry. When he writes, "Under a
spreading chestnut tree/The Village smithy stands," the
poet is referring to the blacksmith's building, the
smithy, and not the blacksmith himself. He gets to the
man himself in the following line, "The smith, a mighty
man is he."

• ■ •

Samuel Clemens was not the first writer to adopt the
name Mark Twain. It had been used previously by
an acquaintance of his, Captain Isaiah Sellers, who
wrote a boating column for a New Orleans newspaper.
Upon Sellers' death, Clemens took the name.

• ■ •

Speaking of Twain, his 1876 novel *The Adventures of Tom Sawyer* was the first ever to be written on a typewriter. The author used a Remington, although no one but his family and publisher knew it at the time; he said later that he kept it a secret because he didn't want to be asked to endorse the machines in advertising.

• ■ •

The line immortalized by Snoopy in the *Peanuts* comic strip, "It was a dark and stormy night," is from Edward Bulwer-Lytton's novel *Paul Clifford* (1830).

• ■ •

Sir Lancelot, a Knight of the Round Table and lover of Guinevere in the legends of King Arthur, was neither. Though a real Arthur apparently lived in the 6th century A.D., and poems about him sprung up roughly a century later, Lancelot made his debut in a fictional French story written in the late 12th century. In *Lancelot* (1170) he is in love with Guinevere—but nothing comes of it. He didn't become a member of Arthur's court, in literature, until the 14th century, presumably placed there by scribes who didn't realize (or didn't care) that *Lancelot* was fiction.

• ■ •

Alfred, Lord Tennyson's immortal lament, " 'Tis better to have loved and lost/Than never to have loved at all" was written to a man. The lines, from his poem *In Memoriam,* were written of his dear young friend Arthur Hallam, who died when he was 22.

• ■ •

There really was a Mary who inspired the 1830 poem "Mary Had a Little Lamb." Editor Sarah Josepha Hale wrote the poem for her *Godey's Ladies' Magazine* when she saw little Mary Tyler's pet lamb following her to school one day . . . which was against the rules.

• ■ •

Clark Kent was named after actors Clark Gable and Kent Taylor. His creators, Jerry Siegel and Joe Shuster, were 16-years-olds who lived in Cleveland; they conceived the story as a comic strip, which was rejected by 15 syndicates before it finally found a home in the fledgling comic book industry. The rest is history.

Incidentally, when Superman was first introduced, he couldn't fly and wasn't invulnerable. He was strong and resilient, all right, but he was just as his name suggests: a super man who could "leap tall buildings in a single bound."

• ■ •

The real first name of science fiction hero Buck Rogers is Anthony.

• ■ •

The maiden name of comic book character Blondie is Boopadoop. She is the wife of Dagwood Bumstead; they were married in 1933.

The Military

Given the military's fondness for redundancies, it should come as no surprise that the "D" in D-Day stands for "Day." Like H-Hour, it's standard military usage that predates the Allied invasion of June 6, 1944.

• ■ •

Why is "colonel" pronounced "kernel"? Because it's an odd hybrid. The pronunciation is based on the Spanish *coronel* (we dropped the middle "o" circa 1800), while the spelling comes from the Italian *colonnello*, which derives from *colonna* ("column,") and -*ello*, ("little,")—a "little column," which is what a colonel leads into battle.

• ■ •

Apart from humans, the only creatures that go into battle in formation are ants.

• ■ •

It really happened: during the Civil War, the Union's General John Sedgwick was in Spotsylvania, Virginia, assessing the enemy's strength. After surveying the situation, he turned to an aide and with a snicker uttered his last words: "They couldn't hit an elephant at this dist—"

• ■ •

The only American casualties of World War II to die on American soil were a mother and her five children. They were killed in Oregon in 1945 when they moved a live balloon bomb. The bomb was one of nine thousand released by the Japanese; only 85 reached these shores.

• ■ •

The Medal of Honor is the only medal awarded by the U.S. military that is worn around the neck.

• ■ •

A "flash in the pan" has nothing to do with cooking. The "pan" refers to the pan of a gun, and the "flash" was the detonation of the priming powder. If the flash went off without detonating the main charge, it was said to be nothing more than a flash in the pan.

• ■ •

Having "room to swing a cat" has nothing to do with animals. It has to do with military punishment. On naval vessels of the 17th century, when flogging was in flower, the person doing the whipping admonished observers to stand back and give him room to swing his cat o'nine tails.

• ■ •

It was Napoleon's idea to put brass buttons on military uniforms. Slogging through Russia in the dead of winter, he was tired of seeing his soldiers wipe their noses with their sleeves. Brass buttons pulled from the jackets of the dead and sewn onto the sleeves were a way of preventing that.

• ■ •

The term "dud" as applied to any shell that didn't explode was first used by the English in World War I. It was derived from the old English word *dudde* for "rags," or something that failed to meet one's expectations.

• ■ •

The military gave us other words as well. One came about when William the Conqueror told his troops to douse their fires. The French words he used were "*couvre feu*," from whence came the word "curfew."

• ■ •

Then there's "boonies" which comes from "boondocks," for someplace remote and difficult to reach. The phrase originated in the Philippines during World War II, where a local word for mountain was *bundock*.

• ■ •

Paratroopers shouting "Geronimo" originated with Indian soldiers during World War II. Not only was Geronimo famed for launching surprise attacks, but there's a story, possibly apocryphal, that the Apache warrior shouted his own name while jumping off a cliff, pursued by soldiers. The jump should have killed him but didn't, which is why paratroopers began using it.

Motion Pictures, Television, and Radio

Hollywood got its name in 1887 thanks to Daeida Wilcox, whose husband Harvey, of Kansas, owned the land. Hollywood was the name of the summer home of a woman Mrs. Wilcox had sat beside on a train, and she liked the sound of it.

• ■ •

In cartoon reality, vintage flapper girl Betty Boop is only 16 years old.

• ■ •

The first talkie wasn't *The Jazz Singer*. Released in 1927, it was the first film that had talking in it, but most of the film was still silent. Al Jolson starred after fellow Broadway actors George Jessel and Eddie Cantor turned the project down.

The first all-talking movie, *The Lights of New York*, was released the following year.

The first film to feature sound was *Don Juan*, released in 1926, though that one had sound effects only.

• ■ •

Though Bela Lugosi had created the part on stage, Lon Chaney, Sr. was signed to play the role of Dracula in the 1931 film. However, the legendary horror star died of cancer and the role went to Lugosi.

• ■ •

Flushed with success from his film *Dracula*, Lugosi was next offered the part of the Monster in *Frankenstein*. However, when he learned that his distinctive voice wouldn't be used, he turned the role down; enter former truck driver William Henry Pratt, who took the part, took a new name—Boris Karloff—and eclipsed Lugosi as the industry's leading horror star.

• ■ •

Radio hero the Lone Ranger, a.k.a. John Reid, is the great uncle of the Green Hornet, a.k.a. Britt Reid. Writer Fran Striker created both characters.

• ■ •

In 1956, the Oscar for Best Original Screenplay went to the film *The Red Balloon*. The picture hasn't a word of dialogue.

• ■ •

MGM's famous lion logo was created in 1916 for the Goldwyn Pictures Corporation by advertising executive Howard Dietz, a Columbia University graduate, who based it on the school's fight song, "Roar, Lion, Roar." When Goldwyn merged with Metro and Louis B. Mayer in 1924, the lion went along.

The name Leo, of course, comes from the constellation.

• ■ •

Dorothy's ruby slippers aren't. In the original L. Frank Baum novel *The Wonderful Wizard of Oz* (1900) they're silver. But silver wouldn't have photographed as strikingly in Technicolor, so the color was changed to ruby for the 1939 film.

• ■ •

The cartoon characters Rocky and Bullwinkle were named, respectively, for fighters Rocky Graziano and used car salesman Clarence Bulwinkle. Creator Jay Ward admired the former and got a chuckle out of the latter.

• ■ •

Lucy Ricardo's maiden name is MacGillicuddy.

• ■ •

In 1927, actress Norma Talmadge accidentally stepped in wet concrete outside Graumann's Chinese Theater in Hollywood. Owner Sid Graumann left it there and asked other stars to do likewise, figuring it would attract customers to his theater.

He was right. It still does.

• ■ •

Before he became a star of vaudeville, comedian Lou Costello was a movie stuntman. Among his jobs was doubling for actress Delores Del Rio in *Trail of '98* (1929).

• ■ •

Producer David O. Selznick really wanted Paulette Goddard to star as Scarlett O'Hara in *Gone With the Wind*. However, after conducting a highly publicized worldwide talent search, he said it would have been embarrassing to cast someone who was literally his neighbor. He kept looking, and found Vivien Leigh.

• ■ •

Walt Disney originally wanted to call his new mouse "Mortimer," but Mrs. Disney talked him out of it. She suggested "Mickey" instead, and Walt grudgingly agreed.

• ■ •

The newspaper of record, *The New York Times*, wrote the following about TV in 1939: "The problem with television is that the people must sit and keep their eyes glued on a screen; the average American family hasn't time for it. . . . for this reason, if for no other, television will never be a serious competitor of broadcasting."

So there.

Music

After listening to several bands perform in 1962, Decca decided to sign the Tremeloes. The Beatles had to go elsewhere to become famous.

• ■ •

The rumors of secret messages hidden in Beatles tunes began in 1966, when a backward-playing tape was used in "Rain," the B-side of "Paperback Writer." The truth was, John Lennon had put the tape in backward by accident. The sound intrigued the band, so they decided to put it in the song.

• ■ •

The last song Elvis sang in public was "Can't Help Falling in Love." He performed it at his last concert appearance, on June 26, 1977.

• ■ •

Rocker David Bowie was born David Jones, but changed his name to avoid confusion with that of another rock star, Monkees member Davy Jones. As David Jones, Bowie had actually begun recording first, with the King Bees in 1964.

•   ■   •

"The Alphabet Song," "Twinkle, Twinkle Little Star," and "Baa, Baa, Black Sheep" all have the same music, which was written in 1765 for the French song *"Ah! Vous Diraije Maman."*

•   ■   •

In the circa 1700 carol "The Twelve Days of Christmas," the fourth day's gift is "collied" birds (black birds), not "calling" birds. What's more, the five golden rings aren't jewelry but ringed pheasants.

•   ■   •

The Christmas carol that begins, "God rest you merry gentlemen" is usually mispunctuated and missung. The correct phrase is, "God rest you merry, gentlemen." Though the carol was first written down in 1827, it is at least four hundred years older than that. And as used in the 15th century, "merry" meant "pleasantly," which was how the singer hoped the gentlemen rested.

• ■ •

Ross Bagdasarian, creator of the singing Alvin and the Chipmunks, was the cousin of distinguished novelist William Saroyan. Saroyan was a former songwriting partner with his inventive cousin.

Bagdasarian first conceived of the chipmunks after nearly running one over on a country road. He named them Alvin, Simon, and Theodore after a trio of record executives.

• ■ •

According to his baptismal certificate, flag-waving song-and-dance man George M. Cohan was born on the third of July, not on the fourth, in 1878.

• ■ •

Cohan's original title for one of his many great patriotic songs was, "You're a Grand Old Rag." But when the song was published in 1906 there were complaints that Cohan was being disrespectful, so he quietly changed "rag" to "flag."

• ■ •

The real Tom Dooley of the Kingston Trio's 1958 number-one hit was a man named Tom Dula, and he was hanged in North Carolina in 1868 for the murder of his former girlfriend.

• ■ •

In 1948, choreographer Jerome Robbins started working on a musical, inspired by *Romeo and Juliet,* about a Jewish and Catholic family warring over the Easter/-Passover holidays. Composer Leonard Bernstein persuaded him to change the characters to white and Hispanic families, and *East Side Story* became *West Side Story.* The musical eventually reached Broadway in September, 1957.

• ■ •

Singers Paul Simon and Art Garfunkel originally billed themselves Tom and Jerry. Their first single, "Our Song," was released in 1958.

• ■ •

When Paul McCartney recorded his song "Yesterday" in 1965, none of the other Beatles was present; just McCartney on the guitar and a group of string musicians. The song remains the most-recorded in music history.

• ■ •

The Swanee River, immortalized by Stephen Foster in his song "The Old Folks at Home" and by Irving Caesar and George Gershwin in "Swanee," doesn't exist. Foster wrote the song, his first, in 1851. He was in Pittsburgh at the time, and decided that the Pedee River used in his first draft just didn't sound right. He found the Suwannee River in an atlas and shortened the name so it would fit. Caesar and Gershwin reused the popular name in their 1919 song.

• ■ •

The theme of the Confederacy, "Dixie," was actually composed by a black Northerner, Daniel D. Emmett. It was first performed in a Broadway minstrel show in 1860.

• ■ •

When dancer Renee Fladen decided she didn't want to date keyboardist Michael Brown any longer, he wrote a song, recorded it, and had a top-five smash in 1966, "Walk Away Renee," with his band the Left Banke.

Still heartbroken, Brown then wrote the Fladen-inspired "Pretty Ballerina," which was a hit the following year.

• ■ •

Back in pre-Revolutionary America, when the song "Yankee Doodle" was popular, the hero didn't stick a feather in his hat and call it pasta. "Macaroni" referred to a fancy-dressing Italian, a style which at the time was widely imitated in England. By sticking just a feather in his cap and calling himself a natty dresser,

Yankee Doodle was showing himself to be a rube—
which was how the English regarded many colonials at
the time.

• ■ •

The "matilda" of the Australian ditty "Waltzing Matilda" is not a girl but a knapsack. The word "waltz"
meant "trek."

The song was composed in 1895 and, though it was
Australia's unofficial national anthem for many years,
the honor actually belongs to "Advance Australia Fair."

• ■ •

Bagpipes were invented in Iran and were brought to
Britain by the Romans, where they eventually became the national instrument of Scotland.

• ■ •

The popular "River Kwai March" from the 1957
motion picture *The Bridge on the River Kwai* was
actually a marching song called "The Colonel Bogey
March," written in 1916 by Kenneth J. Alford, the
bandmaster of the Second Battalion, Argyll and Suther-
land Highlanders.

Since the POWs apparently hummed (not whistled)
it as they marched into the Japanese camp, director
David Lean used it in his film.

• ■ •

The first music video aired on MTV was "Video Killed the Radio Star" by the Buggles. It was shown at midnight, August 1, 1981. Though MTV was a hit, the song wasn't. The group disbanded the same year.

• ■ •

Frederic Chopin's "Minute Waltz" is not meant to be played in a minute. The composer intended the word to mean "small."

• ■ •

Guitarist Jimmy Page came up with the name Lead Zeppelin for his new band because, he said, "It'll go down like a lead balloon." However, he decided to misspell "lead" as "led" so it wouldn't be mispronounced as "leed."

• ■ •

In the olden days, a "weasel" was a tool used by hatters, and "pop" was slang for "pawn." Thus, when "that's the way the money goes," there is only one option left: "pop goes the weasel."

Odds 'n' Ends

If you add the number of letters in the names of the cards in a deck of cards, excluding the joker, the count is 52—the same as the number of cards in the deck. (We'll save you the trouble of writing it out: acetwothreefourfivesixseveneightninetenjackqueenking.)

• ■ •

Whichever way it's done, U.S. currency can only be folded by hand into six equal folds.

• ■ •

The *Titanic* almost certainly would have made a safe passage if it hadn't been for a cranky radio operator. A passing ship, *The Californian*, warned John George Phillips of the potential danger. However, Phillips was tired, still had dozens of messages to send for passengers, and told *The Californian* to leave him alone. Forty minutes later, at 11:40 p.m. on April 14, 1912, the ship struck an iceberg. Two hours, forty minutes later, the *Titanic* was gone.

• ■ •

What we buy in the post office are not post cards, they're postal cards. Postal cards are the ones that have postage printed on them. Post cards are the ones with pictures.

• ■ •

The name of the Amazons, the race of warrior women battled by Hercules and others, derives from the Greek "a," ("without,") and "mazos," ("breast,"). The women reportedly cut off their right breasts so they'd have greater freedom of movement to wield their weapons.

In 1541, when the explorer Francisco de Orellana found strong and vigorous women living in South America, he assumed that these were the women of legend and dubbed them Amazons.

• ■ •

The ubiquitous yellow smiling face, with its black curve of a mouth and dot eyes, originated as a button giveaway of AM radio station WMCA in 1965. The face was designed to represent the "Good Guy" deejays at the rock station. Unfortunately, the face was never trademarked.

• ■ •

Eyes sometimes seem red in photographs because the flash reflects from the back of the eye, which is thick with blood vessels. You can decrease the redness by having your subjects avert their gaze slightly, or by turning on other lights, which would cause the pupil to dilate and cut down the amount of red light bouncing back.

• ■ •

It's virtually impossible to cover the squares of a chess board with coins. If you double the number of coins on each new square (1, 2, 4, 8, 16, 32, 64, 128, 256, 512, 1024, 2048, 4096, 8192, 16,384, 32,768, 65,536, 131,072, 262,144, 524,288, 1,048,576, 2,097,152, 4,194,304, 8,388,608, 16,777,216, 33,554,432, 67,108,864, etc.) that's over 67 million, and you're not even halfway there! To cover the 64 squares, you'd need over 18 quintillion coins—more than there are or have ever been.

• ■ •

Statistically speaking, 90 percent of us put on our left socks first, while 75 percent of us wash our bellies first when we shower.

• ■ •

When the Romans first invented the mile, it was five thousand feet; that's one thousand paces (two full steps) covering an average of five feet each. The mile gained its extra 280 feet in the 16th century, when the British based their measurements on the length of the average furrow in a field: 660 feet, or a furlong. Furlongs didn't go evenly into miles, so the latter was simply upped until eight of them could fit cleanly.

Outer Space

Due to their eccentric orbits, "ninth planet" Pluto has been the eighth planet from the sun, and Neptune the ninth, since 1979. They will remain so until the year 2113.

• ■ •

Most people know the first words Neil Armstrong said when he stepped onto the moon: "That's one small step for man, one giant leap for mankind." However, you probably don't remember the second words he said on the moon: "The surface is fine and powdery."

Incidentally, Armstrong was so overwhelmed by the event that he blew what he'd intended to say: "That's one small step for *a* man . . ."

• ■ •

The first human voice heard from outer space belonged to President Eisenhower. On December 19, 1958, the recording was beamed to earth from onboard a satellite that had been launched the day before. Eisenhower's message said, "To all mankind, America's wish for peace on earth and good will to men everywhere."

• ■ •

To date, the greatest number of people in space at one time has been eight: five crewmembers onboard the American shuttle *Challenger*, and three cosmonauts on a Soviet craft. It happened in 1984.

• ■ •

It wasn't by whim that scientists launched U.S. space shots from Cape Canaveral, Florida. They wanted to have a lot of ocean for the booster rockets to fall in but, more important, the Cape made it easier for the payloads to reach outer space! The Earth turns from west to east at 910 miles an hour: firing a rocket to the east gives it that much of a head start to the 17,300 miles an hour it must achieve to reach escape velocity.

• ■ •

Despite the fact that they're usually pictured as having a tail, comets get them only when they come near the sun. As the comet approaches, the ice that comprises it begins to burn off, leaving a trail behind it.

• ■ •

Sunspots look black but aren't. They're quite bright, in fact, but are cooler than the surrounding matter and thus appear darker.

Sunspots are solar matter held in place by regions of strong magnetism; some are larger than the earth, and last from several hours to several months.

• ■ •

The sun also sends out bursts of energy called flares. When electrically charged particles from these flares reach the earth's atmosphere, they glow, creating the aurora borealis, the northern lights, or the aurora australis, the southern lights.

• ■ •

Trekkers, take note: many scientists once believed there was a planet named Vulcan located between Mercury and the sun. The planet's existence was first hypothesized by Urbain Jean Joseph Leverrier in 1845, when perturbations in Mercury's orbit could only be explained, he thought, by the gravitational tug of an inner body. Another scientist even claimed to have seen Vulcan (it was probably an asteroid).

Einstein's theory of relativity later explained the irregularities in Mercury's orbit as being perfectly natural.

End of Vulcan.

Plants

Poison ivy climbs like ivy but isn't; poison oak is often found on oak, but isn't oak. Both are anacardiaceous shrubs, members of the cashew family.

And if you think poison ivy and cashews are strange bedfellows, the onion and the lily also belong to the same family.

• ■ •

The angle between a tree's trunk and its major branches is the same as the angle between the main vein in its leaves and the smaller arteries.

• ■ •

Mushrooms don't really grow overnight or after a heavy rain. Since they live close to the surface of the ground, they simply swell to a much greater size thanks to rain or heavy dew.

• ▪ •

Banana oil doesn't come from bananas; the fruit does not produce oil of any kind. Banana oil is an artificial mixture which happens to smell like bananas.

Science

A fan doesn't cool a room; in fact, it raises room temperature several degrees because of the heat produced by the motor. What makes a person feel cooler is the movement of the air across the skin, which hastens the evaporation of perspiration, thus lowering body temperature slightly.

● ■ ●

In October, 1947, Chuck Yeager was the first man to break the sound barrier, onboard his XS-1 aircraft. The first woman to perform this feat was Jacqueline Cochran, who did it in 1953 at the controls of an F-86.

● ■ ●

Bubbles rise only as long as the air inside them is warmer than the air around them. Hot air rises, after all. When it cools, the bubbles fall.

Bubbles don't pop because of unequal air pressure, but because the soap in the bubble sinks to the bottom and the added weight there literally pulls them apart.

• ■ •

Hot liquids cause glass to crack only when the thickness of the glass is uneven. The molecules of the glass move rapidly when heated. In a cheaply made glass, when an expanding section meets a thicker section, the latter won't expand as quickly. Thus, the thin section will break away from, rather than adhere to, the thicker portion.

• ■ •

Who decided that there should be 60 seconds in a minute and 60 minutes in an hour? The ancient Sumerians did. In 2400 B.C., they were the first to divide a circle into 360 degrees, each degree into 60 minutes, and each minute into 60 seconds. When the clock was invented, its round face lent itself to this sexagesimal system.

• ■ •

Gasoline doesn't freeze. At temperatures below −180 degrees Ferenheit, it turns into a gummy substance. But it never becomes totally solid.

• ■ •

A whip cracks audibly only when the tip is moving fast enough to break the sound barrier. But why does that cause a sound? Because any moving object produces shock waves that move ahead of it, waves that are most intense at the speed of sound. When this conical, high-pressure wave heads through the low pressure air around it, the latter is thrown into violent motion where the two intersect. The result is a loud pop or explosion.

Sports

The first competition in the world's first Olympic games, held in 776 B.C., was a foot race. The participants were all males, and they ran in the nude.

• ◾ •

The name "Brooklyn Dodgers" was not inspired by the players' skills on the field but from the expression "Trolley Dodgers," describing one's ability to move easily through traffic in the trolley-congested borough.

• ◾ •

The first letters for college sports were handed out in 1904 to seniors on the University of Chicago football team. The players each received a blanket with a big "C" on it.

• ◾ •

The event: a 1922 doubleheader between the St. Louis Cardinals and the Chicago Cubs. During the

138

break between the games, Max Flack of the Cubs and Cliff Heathcote of the Cardinals were traded . . . to the opposing teams. When the second game began, the players took the field for their new teams. It was the only time that kind of swap has taken place.

In 1982, Joel Youngblood one-upped them as he became the first player to score *hits* for two different teams the same day: for the New York Mets on the afternoon of August 4, and then for the Montreal Expos that night.

• ■ •

Baseball players have Babe Ruth to thank for the pinstripe design on their uniforms. By 1925 he'd become so fat—weighing 260 pounds—that Yankees owner Jacob Ruppert ordered the thin stripes put on the uniforms to make the Bambino look thinner.

• ■ •

On August 21, 1887, pitcher Dan Casey of the Philadelphia Phillies struck out in the ninth inning of a game against the New York Giants. His failure to pull the game out for the team inspired Ernest Lawrence Thayer to compose his poem *Casey at the Bat,* which was first published in *The San Francisco Examiner* the following year.

• ■ •

Cooperstown, home of the Baseball Hall of Fame, was named for settler William Cooper, the father of novelist James Fenimore Cooper.

• ■ •

Why is a marathon 26 miles, 385 yards long? Because that was the distance between Windsor Castle and the royal box in the stadium of London, where the 1908 Olympic games were held, which is when the distance was finally standardized. The original marathon was 22 miles, 1,470 yards, run by the Greek soldier Pheidippides in 490 B.C., who was carrying news to Athens that the Greeks had defeated the Persians on the Plain of Marathon.

• ■ •

It's possible to strike out four batters in one inning; eighteen major league pitchers have done it. It happens when a third strike is called but the catcher drops the ball, thus allowing the batter to walk.

• ■ •

Athletic supporters were introduced in 1874 to help protect bicycle riders as they pedaled over cobblestone roads. The term "jock strap" comes from these early "bicycle jockeys."

• ■ •

Got a hockey rink that needs to become a basketball court? It takes an average of two hours for the ice in a rink to be semi-melted via a network of internal tubes, removed in chunks by a tractor, and covered with plywood planks for the cagers. The same tubes are used to refreeze the ice, though this reverse process—which includes lacing the ice with powder so it's not transparent, and painting on the lines—can take up to 12 hours.

• ■ •

Football's San Diego Chargers were not named after "charge" as in a military charge. They were named after charge cards. Their original owner, Barron Hilton, was also the Carte Blanche baron.

• ■ •

The seventh inning stretch, which comes just before the home team bats, has nothing to do with the players getting tired by then (a couple of long innings would leave them exhausted much earlier!), or fans needing to take a break themselves (ditto!). It simply has to do with the fact that seven is considered a lucky number.

• ■ •

The term "rookie" for a first-year player comes from the military use of the word. It originated during the Civil War, when there was a huge influx of new soldiers, i.e., recruits or "reckies."

• ■ •

In baseball, there are six ways a batter can get to first base without hitting the ball: collecting four balls for a walk; being struck by a pitch; the catcher interfering with the batter; the catcher dropping the ball on strike three; a pitched ball becoming caught in the umpire's mask or accoutrements; and a ball leaving the field when thrown by the pitcher.

• ■ •

How in the world did tennis players ever become "seeded"? Early in the game's history, good players were given spots in tournaments by virtue of their talents and/or reputations. In other words, those spots were graciously "ceded" by other players. With the flowering of tennis, the word was somehow mangled.

• ■ •

The scoring in tennis is also unusual, though it wasn't considered so back in the 17th century. Early forms of the game were played for silver pieces, each of which was worth 60 sous. Wagers were placed in quarters thereof: 15, 30, 45, and 60.

The gambling aspect was eventually phased out, 45

became 40 (it was easier to say), and the scoring became what it is today.

As for "love," that came from *l'oeuf*, which is French for "the egg," or zero.

Toys and Games

It was the Spanish who gave us the word "clubs" for the card suit that is clearly comprised of clovers. Actually, the French and English helped. The latter adapted their playing card from French designs, but they took the name "club," "*basto*," from Spanish cards, which actually *had* club designs on the cards.

No one knows why this happened, though some scholars suggest that many people resented the use of the clover, a religious symbol (see entry for "four-leaf clover," p. 41), on a game. Rather than change the cards, the English simply called them clubs.

• ■ •

First developed in the Philippines around 1500, the Yo-Yo was originally a weapon consisting of a four-pound stone attached to a cord some twenty feet long. In 1929, it was transformed into a plaything by toymaker Louis Marx. His Yo-Yos were made of wood, and the name is a trademark. Plastic Yo-Yos were introduced in the late 1950s.

• ■ •

The first Frisbees weren't weapons but pie tins. Yale University students began tossing Frisbie's Pie Company tins back and forth in 1947. Twenty-one years later, Fred Morrison of the Wham-O Company saw them still doing this (well, they were different kids) and came up with a plastic version of the flying disc, which were marketed as Frisbees.

• ■ •

The game of pool evolved from billiards in the 19th century, though the name itself came from another pursuit entirely. Men played billiards while waiting for the results of horse races. Many of these men partook in pool-betting on the horses, that is, pooling their money in order to win (if they won at all) a geometrically greater return. The money was usually counted out on the table, which became the pool table.

• ■ •

Toy trolls, which first went on sale in 1963 and are presently enjoying a renaissance, were originally called Dammit Dolls—though not for reasons you might think. The first one was originally created by Danish woodcarver Thomas Dam, who didn't have enough money to buy a birthday gift for his daughter. A toyshop owner noticed the girl carrying the doll and commissioned Dam to make more for his shop. The rest is history.

(Dam was flush enough to buy his daughter presents thereafter, but continued to carve her dolls instead.)

• ■ •

Rubik's Cube, designed in 1974 by architectural professor Erno Rubik, has 43,252,003,274,489,856,000 possible combinations. That's 43 quintillion-plus.

• ■ •

In 1952, Mr. Potato Head became the first toy advertised on national television.

• ■ •

The Barbie doll, introduced on March 1, 1959, was named after designer Ruth Handler's daughter. Unknown to Handler, however, prototypes of the nation's first correctly proportioned doll were made using molds from a German doll named Lilli—a popular cartoon prostitute!

Sears, among others, refused to stock the original Barbies, feeling that they were just too sexy.

When the dolls took off for Mattel, rival Hasbro created the G.I. Joe doll for boys.

• ■ •

Simple Simon is not named after the character in the Mother Goose nursery rhyme. It's named after a Simon who worked as a social director in a Catskill Mountains resort in the early 1900s. He entertained crowds with the mid-19th-century English game Wiggle-Waggle, calling it Do This, Do That. The way he played it, the game was deceptively easy at the beginning, causing people to complain, "That's simple, Simon." He did that to set them up, of course: when someone complained, he would ask them to tell him why it was simple. When they answered, they were out. After that, no one messed with Simon.

The game later came to be known as Simon Says.

• ■ •

Tinkertoys were invented in 1914 by tombstone cutter Charles Pajeau, who watched with fascination as a group of children constructed geometric shapes using pencils and wooden spools.

• ■ •

Another successful construction toy, Lincoln Logs, was invented several years later by Frank Lloyd Wright's son John. He was with his father in Japan, watching the construction of the Imperial Palace Hotel, when the idea came to him. When he returned to the U.S., he began marketing his invention, which not only had enormous play value but appealed to consumers' patriotism.

U.S. History

Christopher Columbus set sail from Palos, Spain, on August 3, 1492. The cost of the entire expedition was seven thousand dollars, the ships costing nearly half that amount.

Columbus's fee for the entire journey was $300.

• ■ •

The first European explorer known to have visited the North American continent was John Cabot, an Englishman who reached Canada in June of 1497. It is believed, but cannot be proven, that Norse mariner Leif Ericson reached the continent circa 1000.

• ■ •

In 1507, cartographer Martin Waldseemuller printed a map which first gave the name America to our continent. The reason he named it after the man who mapped it, Amerigo Vespucci, rather than after Christopher Columbus was simple: Columbus explored the Bahamas, but never during his four voyages did he set foot on the continent itself. Vespucci had, in 1497.

Waldseemuller was aware of John Cabot, but felt Vespucci deserved the honor.

· ■ ·

Plymouth Rock was named after Plymouth, England, from which the Pilgrims set sail onboard the Mayflower in September, 1620.

· ■ ·

It might seem curious that the Pilgrims settled in relatively harsh New England-to-be rather than in the south. The truth is, they hadn't planned it that way. But they were off-course and out of food and drink when they reached land, so the future Massachusetts became their home.

· ■ ·

On September 4, 1609, Henry Hudson was the first European to set foot on Manhattan Island, which Peter Minuit of the Dutch West India Trading Company did indeed buy from the Carnarsee Indians in 1626 for the equivalent of twenty-four dollars.

What is lesser known, however, is that the Bronx was sold to Jonas Bronck twelve years later for four hundred beads, the equivalent of eighteen dollars; perhaps beginning the tradition of everything being more expensive in Manhattan.

• ■ •

What you probably didn't realize about the Boston Tea Party of December, 1773, is that the colonists inadvertently chose low tide for their party. Instead of going "kerplunk" and drifting off to sea, the nearly 350 crates piled up in the shallow water. Thus, it was necessary for the men to leap into the water and smash the crates open, to make absolutely sure all the tea was ruined.

The tea was unusable, but the effect was hardly as dramatic as the "Indians" had hoped.

• ■ •

Though the resolution for independence was adopted by Congress on July 2, 1776, and most members had signed the declaration by August 6, a few who were absent from Philadelphia didn't get the chance. One member of congress, Thomas McKean, didn't get around to it until 1781, while one of the five men who served on the declaration committee, Robert Livingston, never signed it at all!

The name United States wasn't officially adopted until September 9, 1776. Until then, we were still the United Colonies.

• ■ •

Nathan Hale's last words were not "I only regret that I have but one life to lose for my country." According to the recently discovered diary of Capt. Frederick MacKenzie, who was present at the hanging, Hale said, "It is the duty of every good officer to obey any orders given him by his commander-in-chief." The more dramatic words were obviously put in his mouth by someone who had read Joseph Addison's *Cato*, wherein a character declares, "What pity is it that we can die but once to serve our country!"

• ■ •

In 1775, Paul Revere was captured by the British less than an hour into his famous ride. Henry Wadsworth Longfellow notwithstanding, it was fellow riders Bill Dawes and Samuel Prescott who made it all the way from Boston to Concord to let the Americans know the British were coming.

• ■ •

From 1784–1788, 25,000 people lived in the aspiring state of Franklin, settled by pioneers who crossed the Blue Ridge Mountains from North Carolina and named in honor of Benjamin Franklin. John Sevier was the state's first governor.

However, North Carolina needed taxes from its former territory, and Congress obligingly refused to accord Franklin official statehood. By 1789, a pro-North Carolina movement had grown in the would-be state and it returned to the fold. Eventually, it split off again as part of Tennessee.

• ■ •

The Department of Foreign Affairs was the first cabinet department. It was created in 1789, and later became the State Department.

• ■ •

The U.S. government borrowed money for the first time in 1789. They needed it to pay the President and Congress. The total came to just over $190,000; the interest-free debt was quickly repaid, with just an $8 service charge.

Eat your heart out, President Clinton.

• ■ •

According to the first U.S. census, taken in 1790, the population of the 13 states and neighboring territories was four million.

• ■ •

The Pony Express carried mail roughly 1,800 miles, between St. Joseph, Missouri, and Sacramento, California. For all its fame, however, the service lasted only from April, 1860, to October, 1861; the completion of transcontinental telegraph rendered it obsolete.

• ■ •

Jefferson Davis wasn't the Provisional Congress of the Confederacy's first choice for President. They initially asked Georgia Congressman Alexander Stephens to serve; he declined, however, not wishing to be the one "to strike the first blow" against the Union.

•   ■   •

Abner Doubleday, the man who is credited with having invented baseball (he actually adapted it from other games) was also the first Union soldier to fire a shot during the Civil War. His bullet flew in defense of Ft. Sumter. As far as we know, no one was struck.

•   ■   •

The first casualty of the Civil War was killed by friendly fire, in a manner of speaking. No one was killed when the Confederates shelled the Union's Fort Sumter in Charleston, S.C., or when Abner and his comrades shot back. Afterward, however, a Southern cannon exploded and Private Dan Hough was killed.

•   ■   •

Although the famous Civil War battle between ironclads took place on March 9, 1862, it was not between the *Monitor* and the *Merrimack* but between the *Monitor* and the *Virginia. Merrimack* was the name of a Union frigate which had been burned and abandoned the year before; it was reclaimed by the Confederates, turned into the ironclad, and rechristened. The ship's old name was used in some accounts of the battle simply because "the *Monitor* and the *Merrimack*" was more mellifluous.

• ■ •

When the Union's Admiral Farragut shouted, "Damn the torpedoes—full speed ahead!" during the battle of Mobile Bay in August, 1864, he was not referring to self-propelled torpedoes, which had not yet been invented. Rather, he was talking about enemy mines . . . in this case, beer kegs filled with gunpowder.

• ■ •

The Confederacy's northernmost foray was to Vermont. On October 19, 1864, soldiers hit three banks in St. Albans, made off with $200,000, then fled to Canada for sanctuary.

• ■ •

The greatest number of Civil War battles was fought in Virginia: there were 26 major engagements, and over 480 smaller ones. Almost all of the major battlefields are accessible to motorists.

• ■ •

Before the Civil War, the average work week was six days, eleven hours a day, and there was no such thing as minimum wage.

• ■ •

The Secret Service was originally established as a division of the U.S. Treasury Department. Founded on July 5, 1865—ironically, less than three months after the assassination of President Lincoln—its job was to sniff out counterfeiters. Today, roughly 60 percent of its work is currency-related. The job of protecting the President wasn't begun until the administration of Teddy Roosevelt, after three Presidents had already been assasssinated.

• ■ •

The feud between the Kentucky families the Hatfields and the McCoys began over alleged pig-stealing in 1861. The war lasted 20 years, resulted in at least a dozen deaths, and ended only when two family members were wed. The last survivor of the feud died in 1891.

• ■ •

The Pledge of Allegiance was written in 1892 to honor not the Fourth of July or the U.S. Centennial, as one might suppose, but the 400th anniversary of Columbus Day! The author was Francis Bellamy, a staff writer for *Youth's Companion*.

• ■ •

Difficult as it is to believe nowadays, the U.S. did not have diplomatic relations with the Soviet Union from 1917, the time of the Revolution, until 1933. After becoming President, Franklin Roosevelt contacted Joseph Stalin to normalize relations.

• ■ •

During World War II, the U.S. military turned to Navajo Indians to send important messages over the Pacific airwaves. Their language, whose words change meaning with pitch and have other uncommon features, utterly befuddled the Japanese. For example, the fairly simple-to-translate Able Baker Charlie became *wollachee shush moasi*; Ant Bear Cat. The word "district" was sent out as "deer ice strict."

• ■ •

In 1953, the scheduled executions of Soviet "spies" Julius and Ethel Rosenberg was stayed by the Supreme Court. Turns out they were due to be executed on June 18, their 14th wedding anniversary.

They were killed—many feel unjustly—the following day.

• ■ •

The U.S. didn't have a duly elected female governor until Ella Grasso won in Connecticut in 1974. The first female to serve as governor, however, was Nellie T. Ross of Wyoming who, in 1924, finished the term of her late husband, William B. Ross.

• ■ •

The stars in the U.S. flag represent the state of the union, but what do the colors stand for? Red is courage, white is purity, and blue stands for justice.

• ■ •

Ohio is the only state with an official flag shaped like a banner.

U. S. Presidents

George Washington was descended from the 12th century's William De Wessyngton who, before he moved to Wessyngton, was William De Hertburn. And how much more appropriate a name would that have been for our nation's capital?

• ■ •

Thomas Jefferson was the first president to shake hands in greeting while in office. Before that, still holding to courtly protocol from Great Britain, both George Washington and John Adams greeeted others with small bows.

• ■ •

Presidents John Adams and John Quincy Adams were father and son, and Theodore and Franklin Roosevelt were fifth cousins. But only one man was both the son of one president and father of another: John Scott Harrison was born in 1804, the son of our ninth president, William Henry Harrison. John's own son, Benjamin, was born in 1833 and became our twenty-third president.

• ■ •

James Madison was the first chief executive to wear trousers. The first three presidents wore knee breeches. The fashion was begun by the French revolutionaries in 1789, who used pants as one way to differentiate themselves from the royalists. Sympathetic Americans, including Madison, quickly adopted the style.

• ■ •

The first president nearly to be assassinated was Andrew Jackson. Painter Richard Lawrence, who believed he was the rightful king of the U.S., confronted Jackson at the Capitol and fired two pistols at him, point blank. Both guns misfired. Lawrence was sent to an insane asylum.

Jackson already carried a bullet, close to his heart, from a duel he'd fought over his wife's honor years before.

• ■ •

Our 15th president, James Buchanan, was the only U.S. president who never married. Grover Cleveland was a bachelor when he ran for the office, but married after he took office.

• ■ •

Virginian John Tyler was the only U.S. president who held a government position in the Confederacy, serving as a congressman.

• ■ •

Abraham Lincoln was the first president to wear a beard. He did so at the suggestion of a 12-year-old girl, Grace Bedell, who thought his face was too thin.

• ■ •

And you thought staunch Republican Arnold Schwarzenegger and his wife, Kennedy clan member Maria Shriver, had it tough!

George Todd, brother of First Lady Mary Todd Lincoln, served in the Confederate Army, as did her half brothers David Todd, Samuel Todd, and Alexander Todd, all three of whom died in battle. Mary's half sister Emilie was married to a Confederate brigadier general, Benjamin Hardin Helm. After his death, Emilie went to live in the White House, kicking and screaming all the way.

• ■ •

Lincoln's Gettysburg Address was not written on the back of an envelope, nor was it composed while the president rode the train to Pennsylvania to honor those who fell in the battle just four months before. He had begun working on the speech on November 8, 1863,

11 days before the address, and wrote at least five drafts, the last of which he fine-tuned on the train.

• ■ •

Abraham Lincoln was the first president to have been born outside the original 13 states. His home, the territory of Illinois, was created in 1809.

Martin Van Buren was the first president who was born an American citizen and not a British subject.

• ■ •

At six foot four, Abraham Lincoln was our nation's tallest president. Thomas Jefferson is in second place at six foot two and a half, with George Washington, George Bush, and Bill Clinton tied for third at an even six foot two.

The shortest president was James Madison, who stood five foot four.

At slightly over 100 pounds, Madison was also our lightest president. The heaviest was Howard Taft, who tipped the scales at 332 pounds.

• ■ •

Just before being shot as he sat in a box at Ford's Theater, Abraham Lincoln had taken his wife's hand in his. She felt uneasy and asked her husband what people would think about this public show of affection. His last words were, "They won't think anything about it."

• ■ •

In 1865, after his father was shot, Robert Lincoln, Abraham's eldest son, rushed to the president's bedside. Sixteen years later, he was President James Garfield's secretary of war and was with him at the Washington train station when the president was shot by an assassin. In 1901, Lincoln arrived at the Pan-American Exposition in Buffalo, New York, when William McKinely was shot.

The distraught Lincoln vowed never again to be in the presence of an American president.

• ■ •

Believe it or not, no president ever left the country during his administration until Glover Cleveland did so on a fishing trip, passing beyond the three-mile limit. No president ever visited a foreign country until Theodore Roosevelt went to Panama in 1906. Three years later, he went to Mexico.

Woodrow Wilson was the first president to cross the Atlantic, which he did in 1918.

• ■ •

Woodrow Wilson was the only president who earned a Ph.D. He earned it from Johns Hopkins University in 1886.

• ■ •

Valentine's Day, 1914, was the worst day in Theodore Roosevelt's life; he lost his mother to typhoid fever in the morning, and his wife died after giving birth to his daughter that afternoon.

• ■ •

Until Theodore Roosevelt had it printed on the letterhead, the White House was formally known as the Executive Mansion. Prior to that, the White House was just a nickname.

• ■ •

An assassination attempt against Theodore Roosevelt failed thanks to a long speech. While campaigning for a third term in October, 1912, Roosevelt was shot at close range by a man named John Schrank. The bullet entered Roosevelt's chest, but the fat speech was folded in his pocket and slowed the bullet enough to save his life. Tough Teddy went on to give the speech despite his wound. "It takes more than that to kill a bull moose," he said.

• ■ •

In 1933, Joseph Zangara attempted to shoot President-elect Franklin Roosevelt in Miami. He missed and, instead, assassinated Chicago mayor Anton Cermak. Zangara was executed a month after the crime.

• ■ •

Before President Dwight Eisenhower named it Camp David in 1953, in honor of his grandson, the name of the presidential retreat in Maryland was Shangri-La, after the mountain settlement in James Hilton's novel *Lost Horizon*.

• ■ •

George Washington was the Father of His Country, and Abraham Lincoln is known as the Great Emancipator. But the great one-two punch in American history has to be the nicknames of Chester A. Arthur and his successor, Grover Cleveland, who were known, respectively, as the Dude President and Uncle Jumbo.

The only president who had no nickname was Warren G. Harding.

• ■ •

Only one president was born on the Fourth of July: Calvin Coolidge, in 1872.

• ■ •

John Kennedy was not the youngest man to become president. At 43, he was the youngest man ever to be *elected* president. The youngest man to serve was Theodore Roosevelt, who was the 42-year-old vice-president when William McKinley was assassinated.

Nor was Jacqueline Kennedy, at 31, the youngest first lady. Frances Cleveland was 21, and Julia Taylor was 24.

• ■ •

Jacqueline Kennedy and her children were allowed to remain in the White House for 15 days after the assassination of JFK. During this time, Lyndon Johnson commuted to the Oval Office from the vice-president's residence.

• ■ •

John Kennedy's memorable inaugural address, in which he said, "Ask not what your country can do for you; ask what you can do for your country," was adapted from Oliver Wendell Holmes, who said that we should all "recall what our country has done for each of us, and to ask ourselves what we can do for our country in return"; and President Warren G. Harding, who once said, "We must have a citizenship less concerned about what the government can do for it and more anxious about what it can do for the nation."

For that matter, one of Franklin Roosevelt's most famous utterances, "We have nothing to fear but fear itself," was inspired by Montaigne's 16th-century remark, "The thing of which I have most fear is fear," which Francis Bacon paraphrased in the next century as, "Nothing is terrible except fear itself."

Montaigne probably based his comment on Proverbs 3:25: "Be not afraid of sudden fear."

• ■ •

Presidents from Washington through Grant were paid just $25,000 a year. Since the presidency of Richard Nixon, chief executives have earned $200,000 annually.

• ■ •

Until the modern day, when Presidents Nixon, Ford, Carter, Reagan, Bush, and Clinton are all alive, the record for surviving presidents was from March, 1861, to January, 1862, when Americans enjoyed the counsel of Presidents Van Buren, Tyler, Fillmore, Pierce, Buchanan, and Lincoln.

Weather

The hot, still, dog days of summer, which usually occur in July, have nothing to do with the heat causing dogs to lie around panting. The dog days are named after the Dog Star, Sirius, which rises prominently just before the sun at this time of year.

• ■ •

Rainbows can't appear in the late morning or early afternoon. In order for the sun's rays to refract prismatically through droplets of moisture, the sun has to be within 42 degrees of the horizon.

• ■ •

A person "on cloud nine" is in a state of ecstasy thanks to early 20th-century U.S. Weather Bureau cloud classifications, cloud nine being the highest and wispiest form of cloud. Nowadays, meteorologists call the highest clouds noctilucents—not exactly a term from which popular expressions are born.

• ■ •

Lightning is caused by the buildup of the friction created by the interaction of air and raindrops. Thunder, however, is not a buildup of any kind. It occurs when lightning erupts, heating the air. The air expands quickly, then rushes back into the vacuum created by the expansion. The explosive "whoosh" of this return is the thunder.

•	■	•

Cities tend to be ten degrees hotter than the suburbs—because of the heat generated by the asphalt, sidewalks, and buildings—but some good does come of that, especially during the sweltering summer months. The higher temperatures prevent extreme low-pressure systems from forming, making cities virtually tornado-proof.

•	■	•

Seventy percent of the injuries and fatalities caused by hurricanes are a result of destructive water, not wind.

•	■	•

January 31, 1977, was the first time in the annals of meteorological record-keeping that the 48 contiguous states all had snow on the ground.

World History

Cleopatra wasn't a native Egyptian; she was descended from a long line of Macedonian Greeks who ruled Egypt. There was not a drop of Egyptian blood in her veins.

Moreover, there were a total of seven queens who were called Cleopatra, though only the last is well known to us.

• ■ •

Troy, the city immortalized in Homer's epic *The Iliad*, was actually a small village covering some seven acres. Located in modern-day Turkey, it was also known as Ilium, hence the title of the poem. Troy was razed circa 1200 B.C. and rediscovered in 1871.

• ■ •

Iranians have never called their country Persia; only outsiders have, since the days when the ancient Greeks coined the term from the Iranian province of Pars. To Iranians, the country has always been Iran, though they didn't get touchy about it until the 1930s, when it began appearing in movie newsreels.

Likewise, only foreigners ever called the ancient city Constantinople. The Turks have always called it Istanbul.

• ■ •

In gladiatorial bouts, ancient Romans did not give a thumbs-up gesture if they wanted a fallen gladiator to live. Pointing thumbs down meant that the victor should put his sword point toward the ground, away from his vanquished foe. In pointing up, to the chest, the crowd was indicating that they wanted the loser to die.

The gestures apparently became switched by pilots in the early days of aviation, who signaled thumbs up when they were ready to take to the skies.

• ■ •

The Emperor Nero did not fiddle while Rome burned in 64 A.D. He recited, a cappella, one of his own compositions, "The Sack of Troy," a poem which seemed appropriate under the circumstances.

Though Christians were accused of having set the fire and many were rounded up and burned alive as punishment, rumor has it that Nero ordered the blaze set himself so he could clear land he coveted for the construction of his Golden House. The fire began in a flea market.

• ■ •

Moscow's Red Square was not named for the Communists, as is commonly thought. It was named untold centuries before, due to the color of the soil or the amount of blood spilled there, depending on which Muscovite you ask.

• ■ •

In Medieval Europe, a suntan was regarded as a sign of low birth: only commoners who worked in the fields all day had tanned skin. Nobles remained indoors or were comfortably shaded when they went out.

• ■ •

King John did not sign the Magna Carta at Runnymede, England, in 1215. He affixed his seal to it. Like all monarchs until Henry VII, John couldn't write.

• ■ •

Switzerland isn't a neutral nation due to a long-held interest in pacifism. To the contrary, in the many wars fought in the 1600s and 1700s, Switzerland lost well over one-quarter of its population and one-half of its population of young men. The nation's subsequent pacifism was dictated solely by self-preservation.

• ■ •

King George I, who ruled England from 1714–1727, did not speak English. The German-born king—the great-grandson of James I—came to power by an act of Parliament that bypassed other hereditary claimants. He rather disliked England and didn't bother to learn the language. He spoke French to his cabinet and subjects.

Nearly as unusual is Queen Berengaria of England, who never set foot there. The wife of Richard the Lion-Hearted, she married him in Italy in 1191 when he was involved in the third Crusade. The Queen lived in Italy, Palestine, and France, without ever making it to England. Richard died in 1199.

• ■ •

In July, 1715, after several noisy disturbances in English cities, a new law went into effect stating that if a dozen or more people assembled in one place, authorities could order the group to disburse or face arrest. The law had to be read to such a gathering, from whence came the expression "reading the riot act."

• ■ •

Captain William Bligh, of H.M.S. *Bounty* fame, wasn't a captain at all. At the time of the April, 1789, mutiny he was a 33-year-old lieutenant, who was called captain because he was the man who ran the ship.

Nor did the mutiny ruin him. He and 18 loyal seamen traveled a remarkable 4,000 miles in an open boat and eventually reached the Dutch East Indies and then Great Britain, where he was exonerated of wrongdoing.

Given a new command, he rose to the rank of vice-admiral and was eventually named governor of New South Wales.

Chief mutineer Fletcher Christian, on the other hand, was apparently killed by his own men when he suggested returning to England to face the hangman's noose rather than live in exile.

• ■ •

Marie Antoinette did not say, "Let them eat cake," to poor French people who had no bread. It had been uttered 53 years before, in 1740, by a princess who, according to Jean-Jacques Rousseau in *Confessions*, "when . . . told the peasants had no bread, replied, 'Let them eat cake.' "

Obviously, one of the anti-monarchists familiar with the statement attributed it to the Queen to rouse the populace against her. And successfully, too, since she was beheaded shortly thereafter.

• ■ •

The battle of Waterloo wasn't fought there. Wellington had stayed at Waterloo the night before, and returned to the town after the fight. Napoleon's defeat occurred outside the village of Pancenoit, which was over four miles away.

• ■ •

What is Scotland Yard doing in London, and why isn't it called England Yard? In the tenth century, a Scottish king was given land in London with the provision that he build a castle and live in it a portion of each year. Seven centuries later, when England and Scotland had been united under a common monarch, the land was divided into Greater and Middle Scotland Yard. The London police took up residence there in 1829; today, Scotland Yard describes both the metropolitan police force based there and its many stations.

• ■ •

The father of Communism, Karl Marx, was once a reporter for a capitalistic U.S. newspaper. In 1848, he worked in the London bureau of the New York *Tribune* (later the *Herald Tribune*). His editor was a well-known figure himself: Richard Henry Dana, the author of the 1840 novel *Two Years Before the Mast*.

• ■ •

Joseph Stalin was born Iosif Vissarionovich Dzhugashvili. He chose the new name because of its similarity to *stal*, the Russian word for "steel."

• ■ •

The "bulge" of the Battle of the Bulge, the decisive European showdown of World War II, does not describe a geographic feature. It refers to a 50-mile-wide by 50-mile-deep advance made by the Germans against the Allies in the Ardennes forest of Luxembourg and Belgium in mid-December, 1944. The Allies recovered their lost ground by the end of January, and the last major German offensive was over.

• ■ •

During World War II, the Soviet Union declared war on Japan on August 8, 1945—two days after Hiroshima was A-bombed and six days before the Japanese surrendered. The Soviets wanted to get in on the spoils of the Pacific War without having had to fight in it.

• ■ •

Israel's first prime minister, David Ben-Gurion, was born David Green. He changed his name to Ben-Gurion—"son of a lion cub"—because he liked the Old Testament ring it had.

• ■ •

Before she became Israel's fourth prime minister, Golda Meir was a Milwaukee, Wisconsin, high school teacher.

• ■ •

Until 1971, women in Switzerland did not have the right to vote.

• ■ •

The name "Canada" comes from the Iroquois meaning "Group of Huts."

• ■ •

The Third World is comprised of underdeveloped nations, but who comprises the First and Second Worlds? The industrialized nations of the world are the First World, while the nations of Eastern Europe are referred to as the Second World.